Choice and Consequence

Book One of the Peace River Country Series

Choice and Consequence

Book One of the Peach River Country Series

Vic Lehman

Choice and Consequence

© Vic Lehman 2011

Published by
Lighthouse Christian Publishing
SAN 257-4330
5531 Dufferin Drive
Savage, Minnesota, 55378
United States of America

www.lighthousechristianpublishing.com

This book is dedicated to the pioneers who homesteaded and settled the Peace River Country of Northern Alberta, Canada in the 1930's and 1940's, of whom my parents, Casper and Ruth Lehman and their siblings were a part.

Chapter One
The Problem

Justyn Smyth had a problem. Good looking, with a winsome personality, Justyn was single and had enjoyed his freedom from domestic responsibility throughout the latter part of his 35 years. Of late, however, a void within Justyn was making itself irritably noticeable, causing the independent rancher to begin thinking about sharing his life with someone special. There had to be more to life than mere human existence, not to mention facing all the hardships of life alone. And for whom was he developing this ranch, wrestling it from the challenging countryside?

Certainly a further imputes to these musing was the arrival of the beautiful and self-reliant Ms. Sara Hill. She had settled on a farm, a few miles east of Justyn's spread, about 3 years ago. Sara was a widower and had a teenage daughter named Corrie. No one knew much more about her, other than that, in the three years of living here, she had proven herself to be a solid, hard-working individual who didn't always have time to dress up and look fancy. Most often she was dressed practical while she scraped out a living for herself and her daughter from the stingy soil. No one questioned her success at this venture. She was making ends meet. And no one could help but notice that, when Sara Hill did take time to dress up, she still turned a lot of heads her way.

Now perhaps Justyn's head had been turned more than most, not only by the "dressed up and pretty" side of Sara, but also by the self-reliant tenacity by which she looked after herself and her daughter. Largely because of that strong will, and because of Justyn's own reserve regarding such things, Justyn had been very careful in slowly developing a good, neighborly relationship with both Sara and Corrie. Justyn, and Sara, needed such a gradual building of mutual trust. No love at first sight, flash in the pan overnight romance for either of them. For each of them, commitment was not easily given, but when it was, it would be meant to last.

For Justyn, this commitment would involve taking on a ready-made family. That was a lot of responsibility, from looking after number one to looking out for three. He was in no hurry to rush into what his personal values saw as a lifelong commitment.

Likewise, Sara was not about to risk everything she had built up, especially her self-reliance--she knew she could look after herself--by simply casting her future, and that of Corrie, on just any drifter that came along. Anyone wanting her commitment would have to prove their trustworthiness and contribute to her life, rather than simply take from it. Sara was also not exactly finished grieving the sudden loss of her first husband, who was killed in a fiery truck/train crash. Folks said he fell asleep at the wheel, but no one could say for sure. In any case, there was no life insurance and Sara had been left to raise their eleven-year-old daughter with nothing but a worn out old farm handed down in the family, that no one had farmed for awhile.

By sheer will power, determination and grit, Sara had carved out for herself and Corrie a reasonable living from that run down farm, by raising chickens, a few cattle and horses, and taking in boarders who wanted to experience farm living and home cooking.

Her business was just starting to pay for all the improvements she had made to the place and so she didn't need a man in her life right now to just mess things up again. She could look after herself and Corrie just fine.

But Corrie was a typical teenager, with mood swings and boundless energy. She needed a firm hand and sometimes Sara wished there was another set of hands to back her up or take a turn. And then Corrie was so much easier to get along with when Justyn dropped by. They were always joking and teasing. Corrie didn't have a lot of friends nearby; nor did she open up like that to anyone else, sometimes not even to Sara. So Justyn was handy to have around. Maybe Corrie did need a father, someone like Justyn, to help free her to achieve her greatest potential.

At first Corrie had been very suspicious of, and cautious around, these neighborly visits of Justyn. Now 14 and beginning to blossom into womanhood, boarding house life had taught Corrie quickly to be wary of the reaching and grasping attention of men that seemed to have only one thing in mind. All men were the same, if you just dug deep enough, Corrie reasoned.

So she had totally shunned Justyn at first, doing her best to make him feel uncomfortable when he visited. At first it hadn't taken much to send Justyn packing. In fact, little did she know that there were times when Justyn almost decided to leave for good and never come back. But the challenge of winning her confidence, and that of her mother, kept him coming back for more punishment. Eventually it became more of a game between Corrie and Justyn, to see who could outlast whom. Gradually the interaction changed to warm teasing and cajoling. Corrie was beginning to believe that Justyn was different than other men. That he did really care about her mother and her, and that he wasn't out just to satisfy his own interests. As his acceptance of her became evident, Corrie had slowly lowered her barriers, allowing the iciness to melt away.

Now she considered Justyn a friend, kind of like a fun Uncle with whom to joke and tease. Someone with whom she could just be herself, without needing to remain guarded and aloof. In fact it was a delightful surprise to actually find him to be a male influence that was positive, one that could be trusted. For now, the idea of uncle was safe. Corrie wasn't even ready to begin thinking of "Dad." Though she had noticed a little spark emerging at unguarded times between Justyn and Sara, it was far too scary to think of the relationship going further. Would she loose her friendship with Justyn if he joined the family?

Life has unique twists that often severely test the ties of trust we have built with one another. Justyn was in town on business when he became, unwilling at first, involved in a social gathering being thrown together at the last minute. Someone had brought a hayrack and team of horses to town and it was attracting riders like honey attracts flies. Of course the recruiting efforts of several of Justyn's friends had some influence as well. So before he knew it, Justyn found himself literally cast in the midst of several pretty neighborhood girls. At first he felt self-conscious, since everyone seemed closer to Corrie's age than his, but finally he eased up a bit and began to join in the singing and cajoling. As the ride went on however, one of the young gals began paying particular attention to Justyn. Flattered by the attention of such a pretty young girl and assuming she was "safely attached" to the fellow next to her, Justyn went with the flow and ignored his internal early warning system.

Soon he found himself with his arm around the girl, Karen, laughing and joking along with the rest of them. Then everything happened so quickly it left Justyn in a daze, unsure what to do.

First, he became aware that the fellow next to Karen was not attached to her at all, but was far more interested in one of the other girls. Karen was not, as he had assumed, safely spoken for.

Second, he began to notice that Karen's attention to him was beginning to feel a little too close for comfort. Sure she was nice and everything, but she couldn't hold a candle to the far more mature and self-reliant Sara. What she was stirring in him was simply male/female attraction.

As Justyn was just beginning to plan a way out of his current predicament, the clincher occurred. Someone had found Corrie in town, on an errand for her mother, and insisted she join the fun. As she bounded onto the hayrack she stopped stock still, her eyes taking in at a glance Justyn's arm around Karen, seemingly enjoying her obvious flirtation. As Justyn's eyes met Corrie's, he saw a mixture of pain and disbelief, of betrayal and anger, quickly become replaced by open scorn.

Before Justyn could say a word, Corrie scrambled from the hayrack and dashed to her waiting horse. By the time he freed himself from his clinging appendage, it was too late to catch Corrie and try to explain.

Kicking himself all the way home, Justyn was convinced that all his patient and careful work in building a relationship with Corrie was lost in that one stupid moment. How could he have been so foolish to let those kids draw him in like that? How could he have let pride drag him into accepting such petty affection? It was Sara he was beginning to love, not Karen's fleeting charm. Had he blown it all the way around, not only with Corrie, but also with Sara when she heard Corrie's version of what happened? Had their trust of him been destroyed in that one moment, never to be rebuilt? Justyn Smyth had a problem.

Chapter Two
A Decision is Cast

The year was 1950. Nestled in the rolling hills of the Peace River Country, of Alberta, Canada, homesteading farms had flourished. Originally, the government had provided 160 acres to every man, woman and youth over 18 that applied for it. The only stipulation was that a portion of the land had to be cleared and brought into farming production within three years. By the 1950's, most of these farms were established and had expanded, buying out those neighbors who could not survive this harsh, pioneering life. Clapboard houses had even replaced the log cabins by now, but power, running water and indoor plumbing was still an expensive dream for most settlers.

Justyn Smyth was one of the survivors who was doing well. In addition to his homestead quarter, over time he had acquired three more quarters adjacent to his property, giving him one whole section of land. Not all of this land was conducive for raising crops, as the original owners had discovered. In fact, almost half remained covered with a mixture of underbrush and larger timbers. Yet the natural grassy meadows and stream fed valleys were perfect for raising cattle and horses. Realizing this potential, Justyn had focused his energies in this direction and succeeded, where others had failed. Also of great help was his own homestead, which was productive enough for him to raise the grain needed for his own stock, as well as a little extra to sell as a cash crop each year, to help make ends meet.

Justyn raised Hereford cattle for beef consumption. Many people commented that the white faced red cattle dotting the hillsides were as pretty a picture as anyone could hope to see. Justyn owned about 250 of those red and white dots that roamed his range along the Mighty Peace River.

In addition to cattle, about forty horses grazed contentedly on the rich valley grasses. No one breed was predominant is this herd. Most were a mixture of Appaloosa, American Saddle Bred, Quarter horse and miscellaneous heritage. Yet the ones that were broke to ride served as hardy and capable cow ponies. Each was surefooted and trustworthy, whether crossing a rock studded stream, pursuing an obnoxious cow that insisted on staying outside the fence, or riding in the back of a pickup truck, from one work site to the next.

Justyn really appreciated the horses in his remuda, particularly the big gray that he rode now. As man and horse together picked their way along his range fence line, routinely checking for breaks, Justyn found himself grappling with his inner thoughts. As sometimes happens with a single person who is agitated, Justyn was speaking out loud to his horse as he tried to sort out his mixed up feelings.

"Why did I have to go and do something so stupid?" he upbraided himself. "A man my age should have known better than to play with them kids."

The gray twitched his ears, as if listening to every word his master spoke, and then snorted, as if sharing Justyn's indignation.

"But then again, I didn't purposely do anything wrong. I was just having some good clean fun. Why did Corrie have to show up just at that precise moment? Why did she have to misinterpret what was going on, judge me guilty, and run off before I had a chance to defend myself?"

Justyn's glazed eyes followed the fence line, seeing but not seeing, his experienced body unconsciously matching the movement of his horse. His mind continued to whirl, trying its best to untwist all the mixed emotions and thoughts that he felt.

"And what exactly has Corrie told her Mom?" Justyn fumed. A low branch slapped Justyn's ear, stinging just enough to add fuel to his building anger.

"She has no right to paint a black picture of me before her mother and stifle the relationship we so painstakingly built, all because of one dumb little incident. I suppose neither of them will even speak to me again. Well, maybe that is as it should be," Justyn seethed. "Maybe I am better off without seeing either of them on other than purely cordial terms."

Justyn drew up the reins sharply, more abruptly than needed, and dismounted to remove a large tree branch that had fallen on the fence, causing the top wire to sag just enough that an ambitious cow could jump over it in pursuit of greener grass. Replacing a fencing staple in each fencepost on either side of the snag, Justyn tested the tightness of the wire. Hearing a satisfactory hum from the taunt wire, Justyn remounted and moved on.

The physical work had somewhat relieved his anger and now Justyn began thinking a little more clearly.

"What actually was lost through this innocent foray? Would Corrie, and especially Sara, really give up on him that quickly, without hearing his side of the story? Was the trust he had painstakingly built over the last three years since meeting them, really that fragile?"

Again the big gray snorted and Justyn took it as encouragement to continue perusing this more positive line of thought.

"Now really, I don't even know for sure what Corrie, or Sara, are thinking. I don't even know if Corrie told Sara anything about what she saw, or didn't see. Here I am fuming away, assuming the worst, and maybe there isn't even a real problem." Justyn swatted at a persistent horsefly. "Maybe Corrie got over her judgmental disappointment and didn't even tell her Mom anything about the unfortunate incident. Maybe, just maybe, everything is still okay."

But even as this thought, spoken aloud, reached the twitching ears of the gray, Justyn knew that this idea was far too optimistic. Even if Corrie didn't intend to say anything, Sara would be able to tell something was bothering her. She would not overlook the quiet reserve, but would wait for the right moment to find out what was troubling her only child, the one person in the world she loved the most.

"They will have talked about it, all right. The only questions remaining are, how did Corrie present my actions and how can I share my side of the story, without being overly defensive?"

As Justyn rounded the last corner of the pasture and began heading home an hour later, he still had no idea how to broach the subject with Sara, or if he should even be the one to bring it up first. "Should he go immediately to their place, or bide his time?" Little did he know that this decision was about to be made for him.

As if nature was in accord with Justyn's thoughts, heavy clouds had rolled in on the wings of a rising wind. Lightning flashed in the distance and the responding claps of thunder drew closer. Justyn clenched his knees more tightly around the big gray. Having forgotten his rain slicker, he would have to make a run for it if he was to beat the storm home.

Already eager because he knew they were heading home, and sensing the oncoming storm, the animal responded to the nudge by bursting into a gallop. Horse and rider moved as one, whizzing by trees and fence posts, hurdling fallen trees and dry creek beds that lay as barriers between them and home. It was as if they were racing the very elements of nature, in this mad dash to safety before the downpour hit. They had no way of knowing that their race against time was only just beginning.

Chapter Three
Muddling Through

Corrie had fumed the entire 45-minute ride home. "How could Justyn have been so insensitive, to enjoy that woman's obvious flirtations, right in front of the whole community, including her?! Had he done it on purpose, just to infuriate her? Or had she simply caught him in the act of expressing his real self? Was he really just like all other men she had known, the selfish, grasping type?"

Though she fought against it, such dark thoughts brought tears to her eyes. "Somehow Justyn had to be different from the rest," she thought. "He is my only true friend and has always shown me respect. I can't stand to loose one of the only two caring adults in my life, instantly, right out of the blue. There has to be a way to make sense out of this whole thing; to somehow understand what had appeared as a direct betrayal of Justyn's relationship with her, not to mention the budding romance with her mother."

By the time she arrived home, Corrie's tears of anger and of personal sorrow had subsided. She tried to remove the physical evidence of her tears as well, but that was not so easily done. Even washing her face didn't totally hide the red, puffy eyes.

Corrie spent the first half hour at home trying to avoid her mother while her thoughts continued to rage within her head. "I'm just too confused myself to express my pain and frustration to someone else. Besides, the last thing I want to do is hurt my Mom, even with the truth. And then, where is the truth in this situation? What is the truth about Justyn Smith's character? Am I misjudging him now, or have I misjudged him all along?" Before she knew it, Corrie was fuming again. "There just are no real answers." At least none that made sense and helped all the pieces fit together with what Corrie desperately wanted to believe about Justyn Smith.

***

That night as they sat on the porch, watching the stars blink into place, Sara was aware that Corrie was quieter than usual. "Come to think of it," she mused to herself, "Corrie hasn't been her cheerful self ever since coming home from town. Had something happened to her there that needed talking about?" Sara knew better than to pry, however. Corrie would talk when she was ready, and not before. Any inquisitive questioning would simply drive the silence deeper. Sara would need to actively listen to Corrie's body language, for the correct moment of readiness.

While the thoughts were still fresh in her conscious, she began to pick up little nuances from where Corrie sat, indications that Corrie was trying to muster up the courage to ask something important. First it was the restless sitting, trying to find a comfortable position that refused to be found. Then there was the numerous clearing of the throat, the intake of breath, followed by silence and more shuffling in her chair. Patiently Sara waited and then the question finally escaped from Corrie's throat, although in a high, squeaky voice.

"How do you know what people are really like down deep? How does one really know the truth about someone else?" she asked.

Being careful to encourage further discussion and disclosure, rather than stifling it, Sara replied rather vaguely, "Well, I suppose one would have to get to know that person in a variety of settings."

"But what happens when you think you know someone fairly well and then they go and do something stupid; something that just doesn't fit with what we already know about them?"

"Well, Corrie, no one is always 100% consistent. We all sometimes do silly things that don't fit with who we are. Maybe we are just letting off steam, or blowing off stress by being silly. Sometimes we just make mistakes too, and need to come to God, our friends, or both and ask for forgiveness. No one is perfect."

"Yes, I know," Corrie replied tentatively, "But it is so frustrating and . . . and painful to be disappointed by someone you care about."

"Well, Corrie, when it is a friend that lets us down, they deserve the chance to explain what happened from their perspective. Sometimes what appears on the surface is not what is actually happening at all. True friends confront each other about incongruent actions and gently ask for an explanation. That is part of being accountable to one another, especially as Christians, concerning our behavior."

"I suppose I should at least give him a chance to explain himself," Corrie mumbled to herself, too quietly for her mother to hear.

Interpreting the silence as closure of this important disclosure for now, Sara changed the subject.

"It feels like it's going to rain tonight; perhaps even storm. Let's make sure the livestock is secure in the barn before we turn in for the night."

Mother and daughter walked together into the darkness to check on their various charges. They were partners now in running this farm, and the ties of that partnership were about to be tested. Could they withstand the stress of adversity?

Chapter Four
The Fire

The lightening bolt struck the huge old popular tree in the barnyard with a thundering crash. Having been dead and well dried for years, the old branches crashed to the ground in a shower of sparks and burst into flames. Since the storm's rain had not yet arrived, the long unkempt grass along the fence line, running up to the barn, was dry as tinder. It too, ignited immediately, and, fanned on by the raising wind, greedily burned like a fuse up the fence line toward the old, log barn.

It was the cries of the panicking animals in the barn that brought Sara and Corrie on the run. The loud crash had awoken them and the crackling flames had seemed out of place to their sleep heavy minds, but the cries of helpless animals, their animals, instantly cleared their minds and drew immediate action.

Racing to the barn, which by now was beginning to be engulfed by flames on the west side, both mother and daughter recognized that the fire was too far advanced for them to contain. Their only hope was to set their animals free, in the desperate attempt to spare their lives.

"You untie the horses and milk cow Corrie," yelled Sara over the growing roar of the fire. "I'll open the pig pen and chicken coop." Both raced to set their captives free. Quickly sidestepping the rearing, striking feet of her normally docile saddle pony, Corrie tugged on the rope that tied the little roan mare to the manger. But the animal's incessant pulling had already tightened the knot well beyond what her shaking fingers could untie. Running back out of the stall, Corrie could feel the heat of the fire beginning to permeate the barn. In desperation she grabbed a hatchet struck in a nearby post, again jumped past her mount's flaying feet and drove the blade through the rope and into the manger. The mare stumbled backwards and then stopped, too bewildered to escape. As Corrie slashed free her mother's mount, and then the milk cow, all three animals began milling about inside the barn, too afraid to confront the flames that were beginning to lick around the doorposts of their only exit to freedom. There was only one thing left for Corrie to do. Hurdling herself on the roan as it milled past her, she clung low on the mare's neck and dug in her heels for all she was worth. For a brief second, training overcame fear and the horse plunged out the door, followed closely by her two companions. The short dash ended abruptly at the corral gate, so abruptly that Corrie half jumped, half flew from the mare's bare back. She hit the ground like a rolling ball and was up on her feet again like lightening. Sensing the animals may still not be safe, Corrie thrust open the corral gate and let them escape into the pasture.

Sara had not been as fortunate as Corrie. Some of the pigs, and most of the chickens, refused to be driven from what always had been for them a place of safety. As the barn roof began to drop brightly burning parts of boards like torches on the straw and hay, Sara scrambled out of the burning inferno in order to save herself.

Mother and daughter fell into each other's arms and trembled at the roar of the devouring flames, though the heat made the evening air anything but cold.

Suddenly Corrie shrieked and pointed. The flames, having greedily licked over the entire barn, were now reaching hot fingers through the dry grass toward the house. Clutching Corrie's sleeve, Sara yelled, "Take the old pickup and get Justyn. Honk the horn all the way there and back. If our other neighbors wake up, they will see the flames and come to help!"

For a split second Corrie seemed to hesitate, and Sara screamed even more harshly, "Get him! We need him now! Tell him to bring his tractor and plow."

As Corrie raced to the beat up truck, she glanced back only once. In that moment of time Sara had already dashed to her old tractor, still thankfully hooked up to their two bottom plow, and was trying to coax it to life. The engine of both tractor and truck sputtered to life at the same time and while Corrie careered down the driveway and out onto the road, blaring the horn as she went, Sara began plowing what appeared to be a hopelessly too slow, and too narrow, thread around the house.

"If only I can cut off the ground fuel for those first greedy fingers of fire, perhaps I can stave them off long enough for help to arrive" Sara panted. Praying earnestly, she tried to coax more speed out of the snail like, ancient tractor that was already groaning with the effort of turning up black dirt from this hard packed area.

Sara had completed two loops around the house and was beginning her third when she heard the crash of the barn roof and walls succumbing to the all-consuming flames. As a shower of sparks arouse from the inferno, the rising wind caught them up and blasted them into the nearby trees, still full of dry leaves. In a matter of seconds the sparks turned to flames, crackling and jumping from tree to tree.

Sara glanced at her little ground barrier in dismay. It was far too narrow to contain a wind driven flame. Was it too late? Would the house go, just as the barn had? As this realization struck her with renewed horror, she cast her eyes about in desperation. In that second between still trying and giving up, she heard, above the sound of the flames, the drone of an engine wound to full capacity. Justyn's tractor rounded the corner and he plunged his four-bottom plow into the dirt next to Sara's furrow, immediately doubling the width of her barrier as he came. Off to the right another pickup had arrived. Two neighbors jumped out. One grabbed a chain saw from the truck box, the other an axe, and they raced to begin falling the trees immediately surrounding the house.

"Oh, not my beautiful trees!" wailed Sara, but as the sound came from her lips she knew they were right. The only hope of slowing down the wind driven flames, was to take the tinder fuel out of the air as well. With the up high fuel gone, and the ever- widening barrier on the ground beginning to do its job, there was a slim chance the house could be saved.

Though it took only moments, it seemed to Sara that she had been bouncing round and round on the tractor for hours. With the two machines at work, the barrier was now almost respectable. By now another neighbor had arrived. He ran to the outer rim of the newly turned sod and began a backfire toward the ravaging, approaching flames. Soon two walls of flame roared toward each other, devouring everything in their wake. With a terrifying crash the two walls met, reared high into the air like two fighting stallions, and then crashed to the ground, their food source devoured, their progress powerfully halted. All combustible material within reach of the writhing, dying arms of flame had been consumed.

Almost as an aftermath, the rain portion of the storm silently arrived. It came in separate, big drops at first, each sizzling as they hit the parched, smoldering ground. More and more drops descended, until it came down in torrents. The few remaining open flames scattered across the yard hissed and were extinguished. Soon only the remains of the barn continued to give off wisps of smoke. The barn! How many lives of her animals had been claimed by it?

Wearily clambering down from her tractor, Sara could not help but slump to the now muddy ground. Her adrenaline subsiding, she looked at the devastation around her and no longer could hold back the tears. With the cold and wet, the trauma and the sorrow, all ganging up on her, Sara began to sob so harshly that her whole body shook. Though she had won the battle with the fire, she had also lost, and it was the losses that consumed her now, making her feel defeated, destroyed, hopeless.

Suddenly strong arms scooped her up out of the mud, lightly carried her across the yard and gently placed her on the seat of her own pickup, beside Corrie. Her door was snapped shut without a word from her rescuer while Corrie and Sara fell into each other's arms, relieved that they still had each other safe and sound. Glancing in the rearview mirror, Sara noticed the familiar shoulders of her rescuer dash to a truck behind hers, to escape the pouring rain. Startling warmth escaped her heart at that moment. Though several had helped, she knew that she especially owed Justyn Smyth.

Chapter Five
A Reprieve

Justyn had been wrenched out of a fitful sleep by the relentless pounding on the kitchen door. Even so, he would have ignored it, had it not been for the panic scream screeching out his name. Who could want him so badly this time of night, and in the middle of a thunderstorm?

Hastily pulling on his trousers and, throwing on his shirt, he stumbled to the door, shirt-tails flapping, most buttons still undone. Wrenching his door open, he gaped at a terrified Corrie, her eyes as big as saucers.

"Come quick! Mom needs you! Our barn is on fire. Mom says to bring your tractor and plow!"

While Justyn's foggy mind worked to register what he had just heard, Corrie spun on her heel and raced back to her pickup. Her panic finally ignited Justyn's adrenalin. Before the old pickup cleared the driveway, Justyn had yanked on his boots, crammed his hat on his head, and grabbed a work jacket. His long legs galloping in that awkward gate of cowboys more used to riding than running, he leaped up onto the tractor seat and brought it roaring to life. Backing up quickly to the plow, he had it hitched up in record time, and did his best to hotly pursue the fading taillights of the pickup in the distance. Already he could see an eerie glow in the sky, over where he knew Sara's farmyard stood.

Skipping a few gears in his haste, Justyn soon had the tractor wound out at full trottle in road gear. There was no time to warm the engine up properly. He only hoped the tractor would survive and not fail him now.

Lurching into the farmyard ablaze with firelight, Justyn saw at a glance that the barn was too far gone to save. With the house, however, there still was a chance, if they could just widen the fire ring around it in time.

***

Tossing his drenched cowboy hat to the floor of his neighbor's pickup, Justyn assessed the damage around him, water trickling down his neck and back. Neither of the three men squashed into the pickup said much at first, still awed by the tremendous power and devastation they had just witnessed. Each was thinking in their own mind, "it could have been me. My farm is right next door."

Finally, the older member of the trio volunteered a comment. "Yup, this was a bad one. Could have been worse though. Could have lost the house and some lives too. Sure going to be tough on Sara though. Can't tell yet how many animals she lost in that blaze."

The other neighbor grunted agreement and Justyn muttered, more to himself then the others, "We have to be there for her. She is going to need a lot of help to get over this, not only financially, but emotionally." As he mouthed the words, his mind was spinning. Would she even allow him to help, now that the crisis was over? Would he be seen as a strength to lean on, an instrument of God's caring, to touch her life? Or would she withdraw within herself, and slowly die in defeat? He couldn't bear the thought of her suffering in that way. If only the incident in town wouldn't be a barrier now, when she most needed help.

As the men again lapsed into silence, his mind wondered off down a new direction. Me, an instrument of

God's caring? Where did that idea come from? Sure, I attend church when I can, and I believe in God, but to be used by the Almighty? Was that possible?

His revere was broken by the other neighbors. The driver of the pickup was speaking to him.

"Do you want a ride home Justyn? No sense trying to slosh home in that open tractor of yours. Might as well leave it here until morning."

"Yah, I guess you are right about that. Let me just check to make sure Sara and Corrie are alright about being here alone, before we leave."

Replacing his Stetson, Justyn clamored out of the pickup and lumbered across the yard, the gumbo soil clinging to his boots and building in size with each step. He tapped on the old pickup window and found himself eyeball to eyeball with Corrie, as she edged down the window. Silently reprimanding himself for not having walked around to the other side where Sara sat, he stumbled over his words.

"It's safe now. The rain will finish off any remaining hot spots. Are you two okay?"

It sounded like a dumb question, given the disaster they had just experienced.

While Sara mumbled "Yes, thanks, we'll be alright now" Corrie just starred at Justyn. He couldn't quite make sense of reading the message in her eyes. On the one hand, there were glints of great appreciation for rescuing them, but there was also a hint of something else. Was it distrust, or at least a confused questioning, asking for assurance that she had not seen what she thought she saw in town?

But now was not the time and place to enter such a discussion.

"You will catch your death if you keep standing out there in that rain" came Sara's voice. "Go on home. We'll go in now too, get cleaned up and try to catch some sleep. See you tomorrow, when you come for your tractor."

It was stated as a comment, but did it also contain a hopeful question?

He nodded quickly, dumping water collecting in the brim of his hat down his neck, and then lumbered back to the waiting pickup, trying to kick free of at least some of the mud clinging to his boots. Suddenly he felt weary to the bone. A hot bath sure would feel good about now, but heating all that water would take too long, even on his new oil-burning stove. Best just to get out of these wet duds, towel down and get some sleep. Tomorrow was an important day. He had to pick up his tractor, and, hopefully, a very important friendship.

Chapter Six
One Down, One to Go

News of the widow Hill's misfortune spread around the little town of Valleyview almost as fast as the actual fire had. With each retelling, details were added as to how many animals were lost and how dangerous the fire had been to the whole community. In fact, a rumor had even sprung up concerning possible causes of the fire, an idea other than lightning.

Only one man actually smiled, albeit to him self, when he heard the embellished story. Jack Kane had had his eye on Sara Hill for quite some time, in fact, all three of the years she had lived on the farm just outside of town. Jack was an up and rising businessman in the growing town, and he was always open to expand his holdings to include farmland, especially if it came with a lovely caretaker. Looking around his cluttered home office and bachelor styled residence, he wondered how much a real women could improve its looks. No doubt the cooking would taste better too and having someone else take care of the laundry would be heavenly. Besides, a wife would be good for business. Community people had to trust a realtor, if they were to list their property with him. Marrying and giving the impression of settling down, would cause people to think he was here for the long haul, becoming part of the community. They would be more willing to overlook his land speculation dealings and believe he was working for the common good.

Checking that no one was watching, Jack actually rubbed his hands with glee. And now was the perfect time to offer the newly impoverished widow a strong hand of support and encouragement. Though she had rebuffed his attempted affections in the past, perhaps she would be open to a small loan for rebuilding, a loan he could call in, at his convenience, along with her land and her self. Perhaps if he timed it right, that free loading daughter of hers would be off to school somewhere, or maybe have a job and suite of her own. Jack didn't exactly want two more mouths to feed. One would be quite enough, and he would be well reimbursed by her for his generosity. Didn't the Bible say something about perfect religion involving caring for widows? Then he better hop right to it. Opportunity was starring him in the face, and he was not about to let it slip through his fingers. Should he wait until Sunday, when he made his political appearance at church, to make a show of offering help to the needy widow? No, someone might beat him to it. Best to head right out to the farm now, while the debris still smoldered and the ache was piercingly fresh.

***

Justyn had arrived early the next morning, anxious to have things resolved between he and Corrie, before the potentially cancerous relationship spread to Sara. Upon arriving at the Hill farm, he found a solemn stillness still surrounding the place. Noticing no apparent movement around the house, he resisted going up and knocking on the door. If they happened to still be sleeping, they probably needed all the sleep they could get. Not only the exhaustion of last night but the trauma of seeing the damage by daylight still awaited them.

Justyn glanced toward the blackened timbers of where the barn, hen house and pig -sty had been. Should he spare them some pain by rifling through the debris and counting how much livestock had been lost? He would take on that gruesome task in a heartbeat, if he thought it would help and be welcomed. But knowing Sara's fierce independence, he knew she would need to do it herself. His proceeding without her would be like impinging on her privacy. He could offer to help, when the opportunity presented itself, but right now he better hold off. He didn't need to risk yet another crossing of boundaries.

In the end Justyn chose to go and tinker on his own tractor. First he choose to do quite things, like clean the mud from his plow shears, check the tractor's oil and gas, and visually inspect the engine for any apparent damage from racing the cold engine. Then, when still no activity appeared at the house windows, he allowed himself to become a little louder. He fired up the engine and then immediately shut it off again, making it sound like it had stalled and needed more work. Reaching into his toolbox, on the side of the tractor, he grabbed a wrench and began tightening anything in sight that the adjustable wrench would fit.

Suddenly he caught movement out of the corner of his eye. Calmly replacing the wrench in the toolbox, he turned to find the inquisitive eyes of Corrie upon him. "Oh well, might as well jump in with both feet right off" he thought. "Here goes nothing."

Allowing a faint smile to play on his lips, he verbally reached out with what he hoped was a warm tone, "Good morning Corrie. Did I wake you with my clanging about?"

"You wish," she replied, with some of the old banter back in her voice. "Actually, we have been up for about an hour. Saw you come in, but figured if you didn't have sense enough to come knock on the door, we weren't about to come out and fetch you in."

Then some of the bravado seemed to vanish from her attitude and she looked more like a little, scared girl. "I'm worried, Uncle Justyn." She was using that safe closeness now, signified by the word, Uncle. "I'm worried about Mom. She just sits there by the window and stares out to where the barn used to be. She won't move. I can't even get her to have a cup of coffee. It feels like I have lost her. And then, I . . . I feel like I have lost you too." Now a little bit of fire came back into her voice. "Why in the world were you flirting with Miss Prissy on that hayride. You are old enough to be her father. Are all of you men the same? Just want what makes you feel good?"

Having blurted out her worst fear, she stood trembling slightly and teary eyed, biting her lip. She felt coldly estranged from the only two adults she really cared about.

With a calm somewhat unfamiliar to him, Justyn awkwardly opened his arms and, before he could speak, Corrie burst against him and began weeping on his chest. For a moment he just held her tight. Though his had not been an openly affectionate family, somehow he knew that a fatherly touch was more important right now, than all the words in the world.

When the sobbing diminished to the occasional hiccup, Justyn eased Corrie back a step and looked into her eyes.

"Corrie, lets deal with your two big problems one at a time. First, I want to apologize to you for how I was acting in town the other day. You are right. I allowed myself to become caught up in the foolishness of the group and acted inappropriately. I guess my ego was flattered that someone so young and pretty would pay attention to me. It was nothing more than that. I am so very sorry, Corrie. Will you forgive me?"

Again there was that fleeting look of hesitation. "Believe him" and "Don't trust him" wrestled vigorously within her mind. Just when Justyn was ready to turn blue from holding his breath, a smile began to creep over Corrie's features.

"I forgive you this time, Justyn Smyth. But don't you dare let it happen again. Now, can you come inside for coffee and try to help me with my other problem?"

Chapter Seven
To Trust or Not to Trust

Through bleary eyes Sara perused the scene of devastation before her. For over an hour she had sat at the window, seeing but not seeing, knowing she must go to assess the actual damage, but not finding the strength, or courage, to do so.

Justyn's arrival, once he had stopped his ridiculous banging around and had come inside, had been like a balm to her wounds. Not only had he cheered her up, he had even helped get some breakfast into both of them, not to mention the huge amount he shoveled into himself. And now he stood solidly beside her as they surveyed the carnage before them. Justyn was a good man. She was beginning to enjoy depending on him. But she better guard her heart. No sense getting mushy and killing a good, neighborly relationship.

Taking a deep breath, Sara marched forward resolutely, Justyn matching her stride for stride. "I know Corrie was able to get the horses and cow out of the barn, but I was less fortunate with the pigs and chickens. I guess we better start with them." Nearing the pigpen, she felt both relief and sadness. Of her five hogs, two had somehow survived and were already busy rooting through the ashes for something to eat. The charred forms of the other three were evident in the debris that littered the pen.

Sniffing back the tears and resolving to stay resignedly calm, Sara dimly heard Justyn offer to use his tractor's front-end loader to remove the carcasses. He would dump them in the wooded area east of the pasture and the coyotes would take care of the rest. Since they had not been bled, they could not be used for human consumption.

Nodding her assent, Sara turned from the sickening sight and headed for what was left of the chicken coup. A lack of movement confirmed her worst fears. Any chickens that had escaped the blaze itself had been suffocated by the smoke. All were dead. Perhaps that was just as well. The coup was beyond repair. What remained would need to be torn down and disposed of before a replacement could be built. All that would take time, and money, money she could ill afford.

As this new thought hit home, tears again began to well up in her eyes. How could she afford to rebuild? Corrie and her were just barely making ends meet as it was. They had precious little laid aside. Was this the end then? Would she be forced to give up in defeat?

Almost as if hearing her thoughts, she felt Justyn stiffen at her side. A quick glance up at him revealed that he was not looking at her at all, but he was starring down the driveway, and he obviously did not like what he saw.

Following his gaze, Sara immediately recognized the imposing figure of Jack Kane stepping out of his highly polished Ford Fairlane. While most people drove beat up pickups or old sedan's, Jack somehow managed to drive the best. "He must be rolling in cash," Sara thought wistfully, "and he is rather handsome. I wonder what he is doing out here?"

Almost as if in answer to her musing, Jack called out in that deep baritone voice of his, "Good Morning, Sara, Justyn." The nod at Justyn was somewhat curt as he confidently strode forward and reached out to shake Sara's hand. "I heard about your tragedy only this morning, and had to come right out," he continued smoothly, deftly stepping between Sara and Justyn, taking her elbow and beginning to guide her back toward the house. "How bad is your loss? You will rebuild of course, won't you?"

Taking the cold shoulder as a hint, Justyn stalked off toward his tractor, mumbling all the way under his breath, something about smooth city slickers who preyed on helpless females. Surely Sara saw right through him, didn't she? Well, if she needed his help, she had but to call. In the meantime, he had a job he had promised to do.

Swinging up on the tractor, he flipped on the key and hit the floor starter button. The tractor roared to life and he began to rather forcefully engage the hydraulics to life the front-end loader and the plow. He would need to park the plow out of the way, unhook it and then deal with the burnt hogs. He sure hoped he wouldn't pick up a nail or two in his tires, from the debris. Perhaps, if he was careful, he could push much of the debris to a back corner, out of the way, and then haul the pigs and chickens out to the woods.

**

Meanwhile, Sara and Jack had taken a seat on the porch of the house. Corrie had come out to offer coffee. Then, with a fleeting glance of concern directed towards Justyn's retreating back, she had again retreated into the safe confines of the house. Jack was someone she neither liked, nor trusted. He always had a look of annoyance about him when he spotted her. Like she was in the way, similar to a commodity that was no longer useful or desirable. Well, she would like nothing better than to keep her distance from him and good riddance.

Sara and Jack were quietly conversing about the damage caused by the fire. "I really don't know how I can afford to rebuild," Sara was lamenting. "But I need to have some kind of shelter for the remaining stock, before winter hits. Otherwise they will never survive the harsh cold and winds here." Sara was vividly remembering the forty degrees below zero Fahrenheit days and nights of last winter, which lasted for a week, or even two, at a stretch.

"Surely you have some funds set aside for a rainy day such as this? Or perhaps some investments you can call in?" the calm businesslike tone of Jack inquired, seemingly compassionately.

"No, Corrie and I really have no extra to lean on. We used what little we had to make this place livable to host overnight guests. Business has been slow however, in this small town area, and will be even slower now, with this ugly debris to look at. We just never recovered our investment . . ." her voice trailed off and ended with a slight sniff.

She refused to let her emotions get the best of her in front of this man. He had always admired her drive and independence. Now, in the face of adversity, she would really need to show him the tough stuff from which she was made.

Her drifting thoughts were jerked back by Jack's logical ramblings, "Surely you have relatives, or friends, that would help you out? Or perhaps the lumberyard will extend your credit and the bank will loan you the money for the labor costs involved in rebuilding?" He was sounding quite confident now that suitable arrangements could be worked out.

Though he outdid himself in sounding compassionate, Jack actively began to strategize in his mind how to set the hook. All he had to do was eliminate all other sources of help and he would be free to champion her cause himself. He was almost ready to snag his catch.

Glancing at Sara, he noticed a far off look in her eyes, mingled with pain and regret.

"When John died in that truck/train wreck three years ago, we didn't have two cents to rub together. Because he had been drinking, Insurance refused to pay any of the damage. We had to cover it by selling what little we owned in our rented apartment. We had never gotten ahead enough financially to own any Life Insurance so there was no help there either. All John left us was painful memories, some debts and a slim thread to the inheritance of this farm. When the rest of the family, closer by blood, expressed no interest in it, of course only after discovering its hopelessly run down condition, it was willed to us. This is all we own in the whole world, and now a good chunk of it is gone." Her voice trembled now, but she steeled herself to keep back the threatening tears. Why was she babbling on like this? She had never before told her story to anyone in this community. It was none of their business. Why was she disclosing it now, and to Jack, of all people?

Jack was delighted at the self-disclosure. She was rising to his bait. The time was now for him to set the hook. "I'm so sorry about all your loses. You deserve so much better. If only there was some way I could help!" He paused dramatically, as if in deep thought. "You say this land was willed to you? Then you hold clear title to it?"

She nodded as a tractor rumbled out of the yard and down the road.

"Perhaps I then, could arrange for a small loan!" Jack beamed, as if a sudden inspiration had struck him.

As Sara began to protest, he held up his hands to silence her and insisted on describing his idea.

"After all, I am in the business of buying and selling property. It would not be unusual for me to place borrowed money on some land. With the farm listed as collateral, and my business as the co-sign, I'm sure a small loan could be arranged." Jack refused to allow a look of triumph to erase the concern pasted on his face. My but he was good at playing his hand to his advantage.

"I don't know," Sara hesitated, the noise of the tractor now fading in the distance. "I hate going into debt with no solid source of income from which to pay it back. And to put up the farm, our only home, is very risky. I don't think I am ready for that."

"I'm only offering to help," Jack jumped up hastily, almost too much so, trying to sound hurt. This was not going as well as he had planned. He had hoped her grief would blind Sara to the risk involved in his beautifully woven plan. He had misjudged her shrewdness, however. He saw that now and it only made her all the more appealing to him. Should he force the issue a little more, or back off for now until a more opportune time?

Deciding to build one more bridge, for future crossings, Jack sought to mix solemnity and dignity into his final comments. "We are a community. We need to bail each other out when trouble strikes. We can only get through this tough life, this severe pioneer living, by sticking together."

With a flourish he turned, descended the porch steps and made as if to leave. Then he paused and turned once more, now looking solemnly up at Sara, still on the porch. "I will be honored to help you in any way I can, and I mean in any way." Was that somewhat of a leer on his face, quickly covered by placing his hat on his head? "Remember my offer of a loan. I am there for you, even when you have no one else to turn to."

Standing tall, he gallantly strode to his car and climbed in, being careful to knock off most of the lingering mud from his fancy leather shoes. Sara's eyes followed the car to the road and then allowed them to blur as it turned left and headed to town, the opposite direction Justyn's tractor had headed, with plow and his horse in tow.

Should she trust a man again? Could she? Was that a leer she had glimpsed on Jack's face? If she were to trust a man again, would she start with Jack? Or should it be Justyn?

Chapter Eight
The Dreams of Women and Men

Inside the farmhouse, Corrie seethed the entire time Jack was there, patronizing her mother. Why she detested the man so, she did not know exactly, nor did she really care. Why her mother even gave him the time of day was especially irritating.

Dropping the curtain back in place for about the tenth time of looking out to see if he had left yet, Corrie continued her inner tirade. Get rid of him already, Mom. We have work to do; a huge mess to clean up, buildings to rebuild so life can get back to normal.

In her youthful idealism of unlimited resources, she dreamed of the great ranch they would build. Her Mom and her would construct a huge barn, with ten stalls for the registered quarter horses they would buy and raise. The barn would have a <u>humongous</u> loft, filled with sweet smelling, fresh, soft hay - just right for tumbling in and a wonderful place of refuge in which to hide and just be alone. They would have a farm cat and she would birth her kittens there, those adorable little balls of soft, soft hair, with eyes still closed, they were so newly born.

Corrie's revere was interrupted by the scraping sound of metal on gravel. She glanced again out the front window, remaining shielded by the curtain, to distastefully notice Jack still lingering. She scowled more deeply as she noticed him pat her mother's hand and heard the hum of his suave voice drift through the thin glass. Was he reassuring her, or smothering her, with artificial caring? Corrie couldn't be sure. Either way, his continuing presence brought forth a new surge of anger.

The scraping sound she had heard was coming from the barn site. Using it as a distraction, Corrie scrambled to a side window and located Justyn using his tractor's front-end loader to clear debris from the barn site. He was carefully piling the partially burnt boards and logs in an open spot of the pasture, where they could be safely burned come winter.

Just when she decided to go out and join him, assuming him better company then what was on the front porch, she noticed him get off the tractor and tie something to the bucket of the loader. When she realized it was the dead carcasses of the burnt pigs, she shuttered and quickly turned away. Maybe she would just let him deal with that gruesome task all by himself.

Retreating to her room, she tried to distract herself by reading a book, but try as she might, her ears continued to trace the sound of the tractor driving off with its hideous cargo and dumping it in the woods. It then returned, made some final scraping noises as it moved the last of the debris, then idled for a while, just enough time to hook up the plow. Then it headed out the driveway, gained momentum as it hit the road and then the roar of the engine soon faded in the distance.

Well, Corrie mused to herself, with the dirty job done, they could get on with the rebuilding. Where was her mother? They had a lot of planning to do! Had that nosy realtor left yet?

***

Though carefully watching for exposed nails in the burnt boards that might destroy his tractor tires, throughout the cleanup process Justyn found his mind wandering to the duo on the front porch. What were Sara and Jack talking so long about? How well did they know each other? How close were they really? How long had this relationship been developing, right under his nose? The unanswered questions fueled only more unanswerable queries and Justyn sensed his frustration and, yes, his anger, rising.

But what was there to be angry about? He didn't have any claim on Sara. He had never expressed any romantic interest. She was totally free to make her own choices, see whomever she wished. It was a free country. Besides, he was here just as a good neighbor, helping out, wasn't he?

Jumping from the tractor, he forced himself to focus on the dead animals. Tying a chain to the most intact part of each carcass, he then gingerly raised the bucket, lifting them into the air. He then grimly gathered any remaining body parts and threw them into the loader bucket itself. Striding over to the hen house, he grabbed as many chicken legs as he could hold and threw these dangling masses of feathers in the bucket as well. His huge hands completed that job in three trips. Clambering back onto the tractor, Justyn mused how unfortunate no one had thought to chop off the chickens heads right after they died. If they could have been bled, their meat would have been usable. As it was now, only the coyotes would have a feast.

Hauling the coyote banquet off into the woods, Justyn returned only to find Jack still prattling on to Sara. Was that tears in her eyes as she spoke quietly to him? Justyn was a little too far away to tell for sure. Anyway, she didn't seem to even acknowledge his presence; didn't seem to need him, so he might just as well finish up his task and head home. After all, he had his own ranch to run and he had certainly done his part to help out his needy neighbor.

Yet somehow his jaw was still clenched, his teeth gritted, as he hooked up his plow, tied his horse behind it and wound his tractor up to road gear as he hit the farm road. If he was just a good neighbor, nothing more and nothing less, why did it concern him so to leave Sara in the clutches of that land monger? Sure she was a little bit vulnerable right now, but she could still think straight, couldn't she? And where was Corrie hiding? Her presence would at least help break up any inappropriate intensity. Sara just had to make the right decision. What that correct choice was right now, even Justyn himself did not know. All he knew for sure was what the wrong decision was, and it was spelled J-a-c-k.

Chapter Nine
A Glimmer of Hope

The morning dawned clear and bright, but the sun of late Fall did not pack the heat of Spring or Summer. Even the house was chilly as Sara struggled to force herself out from under the goose feather tick that swallowed her in warmth. And besides, why should she get up anyway? There was only one cow to milk and two pigs to feed. The horses could fend for themselves in the pasture. Why get up as early as usual? She would just have to face the ugly black naked trunks of the trees that had once beautified her farmstead. Neighbors had graciously used their work-horses to pull them away from around the house, where they had fallen when sawed off during the fire. Now they lay in a pile, drying. They would make good firewood next winter. Then there was the emptiness of the space where the farm buildings had stood. Thanks to Justyn, that part of the destruction had also been pushed further from sight, but a haunting emptiness remained. How could she run a farm without a barn, a place for the pigs and a chicken coup? She would have to replace at least some of the chickens, if she was to enjoy eggs for breakfast. Buying eggs just seemed too much of an extravagance for her extremely tight budget.

Then there were the ongoing, nagging thoughts in her mind, of which way to turn. Should she borrow money to rebuild? Should she cut her losses, sell the house and land, move elsewhere and start over? Should she just give up? What kind of life could she provide for Corrie and her? Corrie had enough dreams for ten farms but she had no idea of the resources needed to carry out those dreams. In her youthful enthusiasm, nothing was insurmountable. "You just had to get on with it, tackle rebuilding head on" she had insisted.

A whole week had passed since the fire. Much to Corrie's frustration, Sara had done nothing yet about their sad state of affairs. They were just marking time, going through the motions of daily living. Sara knew that, but somehow she could not seem to shift into forward gear. Neutral seemed so much safer. So was staying in a warm bed. But she could already hear Corrie clanking around at the wood stove. Soon she would be in to tear the covers off Sara, if mother didn't beat daughter to it. With a huge sigh, Sara gingerly touched one bare toe to the cold wooden floorboards, than yanked it back into the bed.

Her eyes misted over as she began to rehearse, for at least the thousandths time, her limited options: borrow money from the bank by putting up the farm land as collateral; extend her credit at the lumberyard, backing it up with a lean on the farm; borrow money from Jack, putting the farm and herself it seemed, at his disposal; sell the remaining livestock and seek jobs in town for both her and Corrie. While the latter seemed to hold the least risk to her long-term livelihood, it also held a huge involvement of others in her life. Would she find a job? What would it be like to work for someone else? Would Corrie and her be safe? And then, Corrie still had school to finish. Sara very much wanted her to finish her last two years of High School. That greatly limited the time she would have available to work. How would they cope? How should they try to cope?

Suddenly the object of her musing burst into the room.

"Come on Mom! Just because it's Saturday, are you going to sleep all day? We need to get this place fixed up before Winter hits. The pigs and horses and cow can't live out in the open forever. You have had a whole week to mope around. Now let's get on with it. Where shall we start this morning?"

"How about with breakfast, Miss Energy? You could fix coffee and nice, warm oatmeal. Then bring it to me in bed and I'll just relax a little longer."

"In your dreams, Mom. Seriously though, what are we going to do today? Where should we start?"

Resigning herself to the life of reality, Sara threw back the covers and grabbed for her warm housecoat and slippers. Shrugging into them, she headed for the kitchen, the thought of coffee utmost in her mind.

The fire Corrie had started in the wood stove was crackling nicely, emanating a welcoming bit of warmth. Sara rinsed out the coffee pot, filled it from the pail of well water, and placed it on the hottest part of the stove to boil.

"Corrie, I really don't know either where to begin. Everything is just so overwhelming right now. Should we borrow money and risk loosing the farm, or should I look for work and just sell the animals. That might get us through this winter at least." She purposely avoided saying anything about Corrie also working to bring in extra income. If there was any way she could swing it without Corrie's help, she dearly wanted to guard these few years left of her growing up.

"That's a great idea! You could work and I could run the farm. We wouldn't have to sell any of the animals. I could easily look after them in the morning, before going to school, and in the evening when I get home."

"But Corrie, what about shelter for them? They can't survive these harsh winters without a place to get out of the wind. Any job I might happen to find wouldn't pay enough to feed us and buy lumber, never mind pay people to build a new barn."

"Well Mom, we could just build a simple three sided log lean to over in the trees by the pasture. The trees there would break some of the wind and if we chink the logs, the animals heat would help keep each other warm. I just know it would work. Maybe Justyn could show me how to fit the logs, and help me with the heavier ones, and I just know I could do it. In the early days, pioneers did it all the time, remember? We still can see what they built on some of the farmsteads around here."

What Corrie said did make some sense, at least the part about a log building. There were enough trees around to use, including the un-burnt parts of the ones already cut and piled. But picturing Corrie building it, with just a little help, brought Sara as close to laughter as she had been in a week. Being careful not to hurt Corrie, or squelch the enthusiasm, Sara replied cautiously.

"It would be nice to keep the milk cow, so we have fresh milk to drink every day. And if we could raise a litter of pigs in the Spring, it would provide some income. The horses are handy to have around, especially when we get drifted in and even the school bus can't make it here for days. And even the log building sounds like it has possibilities, but Corrie, you and I have absolutely no clue how to notch logs, much less fit them tightly enough to withstand winter winds on the outside and animals bumping them on the inside. We would still need to hire help."

"But what about Uncle Justyn?" Corrie's eyes were sparkling with the idea now, while Sara took note of the affectionate "uncle" term. "He can build anything and I just know he would be willing to help us. Couldn't we at least ask him what he thinks? Please? " The latter was offered almost as a plea.

"Okay, we will ask him and I will check around town for work. But I can't make any promises beyond that Corrie. How other people respond is beyond my control."

"Can we start checking into both today, Ma? I can be ready in a flash."

Just then the coffee pot began boiling, reminding both of them that there were a few more immediate things that needed to be cared for first, like breakfast, getting dressed and chores. Once daily tasks were out of the way, they could begin to pursue their new adventure.

Chapter Ten
Opportunity Knocking?

Jack's jaw dropped, leaving his mouth in a gape in spite of himself, as he saw Sara approaching him from down the street. He had never seen her look so good, all dressed up in that stylish black squirt and white blouse. The light jacket she wore neither accented, or hid, her stylish figure. Slowly closing his mouth, and trying to clear the lust from his eyes, Jack waited for her to reach the building where he stood. She appeared to be popping into each store as she came, remaining in each for only a few moments, and never purchasing anything. What was she up to?

Noticing movement on the opposite side of the street, Jack recognized Corrie, following a similar pattern with the stores on that side. At least he thought it was Corrie, but she looked so grown up all dressed to the hilt. Perhaps he had been too hasty in writing her off. She was blossoming into womanhood quite nicely.

Jack was suddenly sidetracked by someone almost bumping into him. It was Sara.

Being the first to recover, Jack quickly blurted out, "Sara, what a delight to see you. My, don't you look lovely today. What is the special occasion? You haven't gone and sold your farm to someone else, have you?" He chuckled at his own brilliant wit.

Having now caught her breath, Sara apologized for having bumped into him. "I'm sorry Jack. I guess I was distracted and didn't see you standing there. No, I haven't sold the farm and it isn't even a special occasion. Corrie and I are in town trying to find a job for me so we dressed up a little. You know, first impressions and all that. So far, it hasn't seemed to have helped any, " she concluded, somewhat wistfully.

In order to give himself time to think, to find a fitting response to this new turn of events, fitting for him that is, Jack began to ramble.

"Yes, with winter coming on, I suppose it is rather difficult to find a shopkeeper willing to take on an extra employee. Things around this little town of Valleyview are not that busy at the best of times, never mind in our "slow season." What type of work are you interested in?"

"Oh, just about anything that pays well enough for Corrie and I to live and keep the farm. I'd give a good day's work for fair pay."

Jack's mind was beginning to roll now, and for a fleeting moment, Sara thought she saw that nasty glint enter and leave his eyes again.

"You know, I just might have the very thing for you. I have been contemplating moving my office from home to a storefront location here on Main street. I could use some help at home organizing and arranging my files and books for the move. Then I would need help arranging the new office, as well as secretarial help once it was up and running. Do you think Valleyview is ready for its own Real Estate office?"

Sara was so totally caught off guard by the implicit offer that she almost missed the actual question asked.

"I have no idea how the town's people would respond. Is there enough business here for you to open an office? We only have a few hundred people, and most business things like that go through Grande Prairie."

"You are right, of course. That is why I have not yet acted on my dream. Give me a few more days to sort things out and see what my investment would be. I'll also bounce my idea off the mayor and a few of the local businessmen. By next weekend I should be able to make a calculated decision."

"Well, I kind of hate to loose a whole week," Sara stammered. "The sooner I have some income, the better."

"I understand completely, " Jack intoned. "Tell you what. You keep on looking and I will pursue my business, and if you are still available when I need you, we will make a deal. How does that sound?"

"That sounds very fair. Thanks for trying to help me out Jack. I appreciate it. I suppose I will see you in church tomorrow?"

"As always" Jack responded. Giving her hand a warm embrace, he headed off down the street.

Sara stood there a moment longer, feeling goose bumps race up and down her back. What was it about him that made her flustered, scared and attracted, all at the same time. She didn't know for sure, but if her luck didn't improve, by the end of next week she may have lots more opportunity to find out, if she ended up working for him.

Tired and foot sore, Sara and Corrie had compared notes on the way home that night. As far as they could tell, between the two of them, they had covered pretty much every business in town with even the remotest possibility of needing to hire someone. A few of the stores thought they might need extra, temporary help around Christmas, but other than that, nothing was available. Then, when Sara mentioned the possibility of working for Jack, Corrie had about blown a fuse. She had made if very clear that under no circumstances did she want her mother near the clutches of that creep, even if they starved to death.

It also didn't help that when they went to Justyn's, both on the way to town and on the way back, he wasn't home. The second time in his yard they had noticed his horse trailer missing, along with his pickup. He probably had gone to a horse auction in one of the neighboring towns. Who knew when he would get back. There would be no dream chasing, building log sheds, that night. Corrie was so disappointed by this combination of events that she had gone to bed early, leaving Sara to worry and fret far into the night, nestled next to the wood stove. Perhaps church in the morning would help her gain perspective. She certainly hoped so. If this faith was so real, where were God's answers? She especially needed sound direction, preferably right now.

Chapter Eleven
"Owe No Man Anything"

The Rev. Tom Alden had gathered together several deacons for a time of prayer in the tiny Sunday School room that doubled as his office. The Sunday morning worship service at the Emmanuel Baptist Church would begin in just a few moments and the pews were filling nicely.

A graying man in his early fifties, Pastor Tom had struggled with an appropriate text for this morning's message. He hated using only individual verses, rather than a whole passage, since he may be accused of preaching out of context. However, this morning he had carefully selected two individual verses, and was planning to link them together to reinforce a principle he needed to present. It had concerned him for quite some time that a number of the families of the congregation, particularly the younger families, seemed to be plunging themselves so deeply into debt in order to establish themselves. While farmland itself was attainable, under reasonable arrangements, it was the farm equipment deemed essential to run these farms that caused the high interest debt load. And it seemed the younger farmers just had to have the latest in farm equipment. There was little willingness to make do with the old horse drawn binders and plows. They needed tractors, not to mention their own harvesters, rather than sharing a threshing machine with their neighbors. Would they ever be able to pay down their big loans? Would they loose not only their fancy machines, but their collateral too, namely the homesteads their parents had chiseled out of this bush-covered prairie? Even now Pastor Tom involuntarily shuttered at that gruesome thought, as he and the deacons bowed their heads to pray.

The singing was worshipful, the children only mildly disturbing with their busy time activities. The quiet books, made from felt or other cloth, were especially helpful to entertain the youngsters. They also saved the hymnals from "loosing pages."

"My text this morning" Pastor Tom began as he prepared to launch into his sermon, "is drawn from Romans Thirteen, verse eight. It reads: "Owe no man any thing, but to love one another; for he that loveth another hath fulfilled the law" (KJV).

Simply reading the text caused a stir among the congregation. Nearly every person there owed money, whether for their home, their vehicle, their business stock or their equipment.

"The pastor couldn't seriously be planning to literally apply this verse to today, could he?" mused Jack. "That would be ridiculous! How could anyone get ahead if they had to pay cash as they went? Besides, my business depends upon people borrowing money, and it is even better for me if they do have trouble paying." Shifting nervously in his seat, Jack continued to speculate on his plans. He hoped to expand his business and more firmly establish a full-fledged Real Estate office right here in Valleyview. With this bud about to blossom, he did not need the pastor scaring potential customers away with some old fashioned view of what the Bible had to say.

"I would like to read one more verse as well" the pastor was continuing, "and then see if we can draw out the significant principle to guide our living for today. The second verse is found in I Corinthians 6:12, which states the following: 'All things are lawful unto me, but all things are not expedient: all things are lawful for me, but I will not be brought under the power of any' (KJV).

"Now what do these two verses have to do with each other? While both were written by Paul, the context of the Romans verse is referring to orderly living and proper conduct of a Christian. In first Corinthians Paul is answering a concern about proper Christian rituals. I would suggest the point of commonality between these two verses has to do with the issue of control. God alone is to be in control of our lives. No person or thing is to take his place.

"I fear for some of us, that we are on the verge of having our debt load in control of our lives. Have we indeed sold our very soul to the proverbial 'country store,' namely to our creditors?"

Sara was fully attentive as the pastor spoke. She had been seeking God's will about the future. Was this her answer? Was she to avoid borrowing the money to rebuild? If so, which other option should she pursue? Was the farm itself beginning to control her? Should she get rid of it too? Would working for others not also place her under their control?

Deep in thought, Sara heard little else of the sermon, or the concluding hymn and closing prayer. She quietly followed Corrie from the sanctuary, more confused than ever about their future.

Chapter Twelve
A Prospect

Justyn had also been deeply stirred by pastor Alden's message but in a significantly different direction. The part of the Romans passage that had stuck with him was the latter portion, actually overlooked by the Pastor. It was the part about "for he that loveth another hath fulfilled the law" (KJV). Other verses identified this "another" as one's neighbor. What exactly did it mean to love one's neighbor? Justyn knew enough about the Bible to know it didn't mean romantic love. It had more to do with unconditional love, like God had for people. This love had something to do with being Christlike to one another. Justyn also vaguely remembered something about perfect religion involving caring for widows and orphans. Was God trying to tell him something about his Christian responsibility to his neighbor? Did he need to love her with a purer motive than "like," and help her out appropriately? He wasn't sure, but he was going to look for an opportunity to help them in some practical, neighborly way.

His opportunity burst upon him sooner than he could expect. Corrie nearly pounced on him as he was about to leave the church yard in his pickup.

"Uncle Justyn, wait!" she shouted. "I need to ask you something."

Shutting off the rumbling engine, Justyn lowered his window all the way and waited for her to clamor up on the running board.

Taking a moment to catch her breath, she blurted out, "Do you know how to build a log cabin?"

Totally mystified, Justyn simply starred at her, having no idea where this question came from or where it was leading.

"Well, not exactly a cabin, but do you know how to notch logs and build solid walls and then fill in the cracks with that stuff?"

The excitement in Corrie's eyes and tone warmed Justyn's heart. Not only did they speak volumes of acceptance, but she was actually inviting his help.

"Now calm down a little and tell me what in the world you are talking about."

Corrie took a deep breath and then tried again. "Mom and I can't afford to build our new barn before winter, so we were wondering about putting together a log shed, as a wind shelter for our animals, to get them through the winter. A three sided shed is all the old timers used to have, isn't it, and they seem to have survived just fine?"

Now Justyn's mind was beginning to buzz with the possibilities of what Corrie was saying. There was enough small timber on their farmstead to build such a structure. Using rails from trees 4-5 inches in diameter would be strong enough, yet easily handled by one or two people. It wouldn't even be that hard to fell enough trees and limb out the necessary lengths. It would be very similar to cutting fence posts, or corral rails, both of which Justyn seemed to be doing on a regular basis. Driving some longer fence posts in on both sides of the log wall, at strategic points, would solidify the structure enough to hold against jostling animals. The only trick would be coming up with a roof structure that wouldn't buckle under the weight of a northern Alberta winter snowfall.

Corrie interrupted his musings with a curt, "Well, what do you think?"

"I think you actually have a workable idea there, Corrie. But your Mom is kind of partial to her trees. Do you think she would allow us to chop down enough to build your livestock a home? She still is having a hard time with the trees she lost to the fire."

"Just as long as you leave the pretty ones, I'll let you harvest whatever you think you need," a soft voice spoke at Corrie's elbow causing both Corrie and Justyn to start. Having escaped Jack's solicitous re-offer of a job beginning the next week, Sara had approached unnoticed and must have overheard at least part of their conversation.

"If you scatter out a tree harvest around the farm-site" she continued, "it should be hardly noticeable from my picture window. Of course you could always plant a few new trees around the house, to help camouflage your efforts." Was that actually a twinkle in her eye?

With a promise to start early the next Saturday morning, the trio parted amiably and headed for home. Finally it felt to each of them that they had something concrete to pursue in rebuilding the farm and, perhaps, their relationship. Was this another answer from God?

Chapter Thirteen
The Job Offer

The following Saturday dawned cool and clear. Though Sara could now see her breath as she did the chores, the sun promised more warmth as it glowed on the horizon.

Hers had been a trying week. After several more days of fruitless job hunting, she had finally given up. There was not a job to be had in the whole town of Valleyview, nor in the larger farm-steads of the area. She had even tried a local beekeeper south of town, but was not considered strong enough to move the full boxes of honey from the hive. He did not need help with the processing of the honey. His large family capably took care of that job.

The only bright spot of the disappointing week was looking forward to this morning. Today they would begin cutting trees and lay at least the lower levels of rails for the cattle shed. In anticipation of this activity, Justyn had been over the day before to level out the selected site with the front-end loader of his tractor. She had been busy canning beans from the garden, so had only briefly pointed out where the shed should go. Justyn had seemed all business anyway as he added his ideas of using the existing trees as a windbreak for the shed. Once the site was agreed upon, both had proceeded with their tasks. He had finished first and left before she could even invite him in for coffee and cake.

As she finished up the chores, Sara was surprised to sense a rising hope within her, as she anticipated the three of them spending a whole day together. What exactly was that neighborly cowboy stirring up within her?

The rhythmic sound of hoof beats interrupted any further self analysis and Sara looked up to see Justyn canter into the yard astride his spirited gray stallion. Sara couldn't help but notice what a striking pair horse and rider made, as she raised her hand to wave. But then, she wasn't interested, was she?

Calling out for Corrie, Sara walked over to where Justyn was carefully dismounting, holding out a large Swede saw at a full arm's length, so that it would not injure the high strung horse, or himself.

"Didn't know if you had a saw or not, so I brought mine along." With a mischievous glint in his eye, Justyn added, "Do you know two Swedish women who could run this thing while I limb the trees and tow them to the building site?"

As he was speaking, Sara noticed a freshly sharpened axe tied to the back of the saddle. A lariat hung from a leather thong on the front, near the saddle horn. One thing about this man, he certainly came prepared.

"I don't know about the Swedish part, but I do know two women who are eager to give that saw a workout," Sara bantered back. "Just make sure you and your horse stay clear cowboy. When we yell 'timber' we mean tree falling your way."

Both were chuckling as Corrie approached, dressed in worn jeans and a plaid work shirt.

"Are you two going to stand there smiling all day or are we going to do some work?" And then, almost as if she needed to get in on something she may have missed, she added, "You must be getting old Uncle Justyn. I thought you would be here at the crack of dawn, ready to go."

The light bantering continued as the trio made their way to the worksite. Once there, Justyn became more serious and took charge, outlining what he had in mind for the building. At first his manor put Sara's back up, but then she realized she needed his knowledge for this project. "Okay, cowboy," she thought, "I'll let you think your running this show, for now." Justyn was explaining how he had purposely cleared a spot among the standing trees so that some of the larger trunks could help support the walls. Particularly butting up the corners to large trees would be strategic, especially if reinforced by fence posts driven into the ground on the inside of the walls, at those same points. The other live trees in the area would also help block some of the blowing and drifting snow that was always so treacherous, and often deadly, in mid winter.

"Now I'll use my horse to drag some of those bigger timbers from the fire over here. They are fairly dry now and will make a great base for each wall. I'll have you practice cutting them to the right length to see if you really can handle this two-man, ah, two person saw. Then we can go and mark trees to be cut, being sure to leave the pretty ones," he glanced directly at Sara with a twinkle in his eye. "If we cut thicker ones first, then thinner ones, we can graduate each level as we lay them. Any questions?"

"Yea, cowboy," Corrie spoke up. "Are you and that puny little horse going to be able to keep up with Mom and I once we hit our stride?"

"Don't listen to her Blue," Justyn said to his horse in a mock hurt tone as he put his foot in the stirrup and lightly sprang up into the saddle. "She is all talk. Why, I

bet we can't get even a half days work out of her before
those toothpick arms give out."

And with a tip of his Stetson and a "Be right back
ladies" Justyn and Blue galloped off to the pile of drying
logs. Choosing the straightest and thickest one, he slipped
the noose of his lariat over the butt end of the log and
tightened it. Winding the other end of the rope around the
saddle horn, he took the reins and led the horse forward to
tighten the rope.

Whether the drying tree was slippery, or Blue just
a little too jumpy, it was hard to say but the moment Blue
felt weight on the other end of the lasso, he lunged
forward as if to bolt. Catching the bridle closer to the bit
in order to stop the animal, Justyn looked back just in
time to see the stretched rope loose its grip on the tree and
come flying at him, the knot striking him directly in the
face, sending his hat sailing.

Just before what may have been colorful words
emerging from his mouth, he heard both Corrie and Sara
burst out laughing. Clamping his mouth into a tight line,
he wasn't sure which stung more, his nose or his pride. It
also took great effort for him to ignore retorting toward
the laughter. Carefully and intentionally recoiling his
rope, Justyn commanded his horse to stand still while he
marched back to the log to reattach the rope. This time he
made sure the loop was higher up on the trunk and
tightened against a ridge where a large branch had been
lobbed off.

Then he calmly walked back to his horse,
retrieved his hat, crushed it back on his head and
commanded sternly "Come on." This time in one smooth
motion the rope tightened and the tree began to move.
Blue skidded it the entire way to the building site,

obediently following his master walking in front of him, who never once looked back, a very serious look on his face.

Mother and daughter tried to stifle their giggles upon seeing that look, but were only partially successful as Justyn approached.

"Okay ladies. Let's see if you cut as well as you cackle" he said rather coolly. Measuring the tree according to where it would need to lay, Justyn hefted the narrower end onto a rotting log nearby and started a notch with the saw blade. Then he turned to the Sara and Corrie expectantly and quipped, "It's all yours."

Feeling a sense that it was now their turn to prove themselves, mother and daughter lined up on either side of the log, grasped their end of the saw and began a rhythmic sea saw back and forth. After a few moments even Justyn could not help but be impressed with how well they worked as a team. Of course, he didn't know they had often cut their firewood this same way, finding this system much easier, and safer, than using only an axe.

The work progressed well after that and by noon everyone was ready for a break, not to mention starved for the picnic lunch prepared earlier that morning. A jovial mood had returned and the easy bantering continued through washing up and setting out the picnic under one of the larger remaining trees.

Suddenly the harsh crunch of tires on gravel interrupted the light family style revelry. As the three heads glanced up as one, Jack's car purred into sight and pulled into the driveway. A matching frown appeared on Corrie and Justyn's face simultaneously, while Sara rose to her feet and went to greet her guest.

"Well hello Jack. What brings you out our way?" Sara greeted warmly, a little two friendly, two minds behind her were thinking.

"I came to bring you good news Sara." Jack glided around his open car door, leaving it open and the engine running, and approached without once taking his eyes off of her.

"Oh, what's that?" Sara countered, with slight hesitation.

"I have decided to take the plunge and open my real estate office on Main street. The doctor's office has additional space available and I have been able to secure if for a decent price. So I am officially offering you a job, Sara, beginning Monday morning. First we will sort through the materials at my house, than relocate them to the new office. You are still interested in the job, aren't you?" The latter comment was made with a barely suppressed hint of desire in his voice.

"Well, yes, I suppose I am," Sara stammered, ignoring the warning bells going off in her mind. "At least I haven't found anything else yet. I suppose . . . "

"Good! Then it's settled" Jack quickly interrupted before she had time to clearly think things through, especially the part about working in his home. "I'll expect you at my house at 8:00 am sharp, Monday morning. Wear something casual because handling files can be a little dusty."

While Sara stumbled over repeating "Monday, 8 o'clock," Jack spun on his heel, jumped into his idling car and drove from the yard, leaving a flurry of dust to drift toward the interrupted picnic.

Sara truthfully didn't know whether to be elated, or worried. The affirmation of finally being hired was exciting but working in close proximity of Jack, on a regular basis, was both appealing and unsettling. It didn't help that both Corrie and Justyn disliked the arrangement, Corrie very verbally and Justyn with stoic silence, as she shared the news with them over the remains of the picnic. Somehow a gloom had settled over the threesome as they returned to what now had suddenly become burdensome work.

The two crews worked separately for most of the afternoon. The women cut down trees, a task they fairly quickly mastered, though quite different from cutting logs lying horizontal. Justyn limbed them, dragged them to the work site with his horse, notched them and lifted the now thinner rails into place. During this time only necessary words were exchanged, such as warnings when a tree was about to fall. By suppertime Justyn found an excuse to take his meal at his own home and he had ridden off with only a brief nod and wave to his coworkers.

That irksome action added to Sara's discomfort. The least she could do to show her appreciation for the man's hard work was to feed him. Now he had eliminated that form of repayment. Was the new job already driving a wedge between her and her supportive neighbor? Would they now drift further apart?

But then, it was her life, Sara reasoned. She needed work and Jack was offering her a job. The money would put food on the table. What could be wrong with that?

Suddenly Sara was startled by an internal jolt. She didn't even know how much the new job paid. There had been no negotiations. Jack had controlled the entire "interview." She knew zero details of the employment, other then when and where to show up.

Well, Sara was not going to stand for a one sided arrangement like that. First thing Monday morning she would demand to know the terms of her employment, whether Jack liked it or not.

With this resolve in mind, Sara prepared her tired and worn out body for bed. However, though her muscles ached from the strenuous activity of the day, her mind, as she lay in bed, simply would not be stilled. Only after several hours did she final drift off into a restless sleep, a sense of foreboding having settled upon even her subconscious.

Chapter 14
The Struggle

The hard physical work of building the livestock shed had been a good diversion for Justyn. Since the building was only three sided, only two corners needed to be notched and fit, as each level of rails was added. The open side of the shed faced south, away from the potentially severe north winds and each end of the side-walls was supported by fence posts being driven into the ground on both sides of the wall. Justyn had made sure to use the thicker, corner post size for this task, to insure additional strength.

By using rail size logs for most of the structure, roughly four to six inches in diameter, he was able to fit them himself, to the thicker first two rows of logs that the three of them had set together. As dusk fell the walls had reached a height of four feet and few gaps showed between the rails, thanks to his builder's skill. Justyn had been especially careful to turn the rails until they fit as tight as possible, occasionally trimming out a bumpy knot here or smoothing out an awkward bend there. Probably no chinking of the rails would even be necessary and, once snow fell, it could be banked up against the outside of the structure, shutting out any wind that might try to blow through. Another two partial days of work should see the structure finished.

Yes, Justyn was pleased with the progress, pleased with helping out his neighbors in a concrete way. But he was greatly displeased with even the thought of Sara working for that snake of a realtor. Justyn tried to rationalize the whole situation. Sara obviously needed a job to make ends meet. Jack seemed the only one willing and able to pay her a wage. Surely the relationship was purely platonic. Jack was simply helping Sara out too, just as he was.

But no matter how he worked it out logically in his mind, Justyn still squirmed whenever he thought of Sara spending the best hours of her day in the presence of that city slicker.

***

In direct proportion to Justyn's silent seething, Corrie was actively verbal. Her agitation, expressly directed toward Sara, was constant.

"How can you even consider working for that creep? Can't you see how he looks at you, or anyone else in a dress for that matter? I don't think you are even safe, being alone with him! And working at his house no less!"

Sara had tried to calm her daughter's anger and fears. She assured Corrie that, once the office was moved, it would be a public place and so be perfectly safe. She had reminded Corrie of the essential income that the job would provide. In the end Sara had become even more determined to see the job through, squelching even her own misgivings.

Corrie, seeing this growing determination, had finally given up and gone to her room to pout. Her parting words were "I still think you should go right up to him at church tomorrow and tell him you have reconsidered and that you won't be taking the job after all." With the last word declared, she had slammed her bedroom door and gone to bed.

Ironically, or conveniently, Jack was not in attendance at church the next day.

Chapter 15
The Job

Monday dawned cloudy and dreary. A cool mist hung in the air and clung to anything that moved through it. The wipers of Sara's old pickup tried to keep the windshield clear, but were only moderately successful, leaving big freezing streaks that Sara had to strain to see through and around. Fortunately the town was still sleepy and quiet as she made her way to the new, expensive subdivision where Jack lived. At precisely 8:00 am. she knocked on his door, determined to be professional in relating to Jack and in negotiating the work agreement.

At her first knock there was no response. She knocked louder and was rewarded by the sound of someone stirring within. Finally the door swung open and she was totally unprepared for what she saw. Jack had come to the door disheveled, looking as if he had just now hurriedly thrown on some rumpled clothes. He smiled somewhat sheepishly and invited her in, mumbling something about his alarm clock not working properly. "Would you mind making coffee and a light breakfast of whatever you can find in the kitchen, while I wash up and make myself more presentable?" he intoned.

This is not going at all like I had planned, Sara mused as she rinsed out the coffee pot, filled it with fresh water and coffee grounds and placed it on the stove to heat. Unable to stand the mess in the kitchen, she began to wash dishes and tidy up before she could even think about preparing breakfast.

While Jack took his sweet time primping, Sara finished cleaning the kitchen, fried bacon and eggs, figured out how to operate the side-opening toaster and set the table. As she placed two steaming cups of coffee on the table, a highly polished Jack entered, sniffed the aroma appreciatively and sighed contentedly.

"Sara, this is absolutely heavenly. I wish all my days could start out this well."

Was there an undertone of double meaning intended? Before Sara could decide, Jack smoothly continued.

"Yes, I just may need to add this to your list of duties, at least as long as we will be working here at the house, or longer if you choose. Now please join me at the table before your delectable efforts become cold."

Sara noticed that no apology was made about the awkward start of her workday, nor for the household chores she had been asked to do. Somewhat reluctantly Sara lowered herself into a chair opposite him. Having already had breakfast at home, she nursed her warm cup of coffee, only slightly surprised that Jack ravenously devoured the breakfast, without even bothering to offer up a prayer of thanks to God.

Collecting her wits, and nerve, Sara plunged ahead with putting her plan back on track, that of firmly negotiating her salary and, she now added pointedly in her mind, her job description.

"Jack, we do need to talk about the tasks you want me to do, and the reimbursement for those tasks."

"Precisely, my dear. As soon as we are finished here, we shall take our refilled coffee mugs over to the glassed in porch. We can enjoy the first rays of the Fall morning sun, each others company and plan our day."

"But I could start . . . "

"All in good time my dear. All in good time. I just love an eager coworker. Pass me the toast, would you please." A glimmer in his eye and the brush of their hands as she handed him the toast made Sara feel a twinge of 'he is hungry for more than toast.' She tried to break the sensuous moment by jumping up to refill their coffee cups. Strange how, though he was the host, she was doing the serving.

Rising to his feet at last, after finishing every last bit of breakfast that she had prepared, Jack offered his arm to Sara and led her to a sun spot in the glassed in porch. An electric space heater had already taken the chill from the room and the lounge chairs felt at least somewhat warmed by the morning sun.

As they were seated in what felt to Sara like a glassed in stage for the neighborhood, Mrs. Talkaday came walking by on the sidewalk outside the right window, taking her dog for a morning stroll. She appeared startled at first, when she noticed Sara sitting there with Jack, and somewhat hesitantly returned their wave. Then she scurried out of sight and Sara could only guess what stories Mrs. Talkaday would tell about what she had seen.

"Now I noticed you didn't eat anything this morning," Jack was saying. "I assume that means you had breakfast before you came?"

"Yes," Sara finally responded, having become somewhat puzzled and strangely uneasy at Mrs. Talkaday's curious response to her presence in Jack's home. "Corrie and I have breakfast together before she catches the bus for school."

"Well far be it from me to interrupt family ritual, but you would be welcome to join me for breakfast each morning." And without missing a beat he added, "I will be more diligent in being ready for your arrival, however. In any case, I would be delighted to provide the groceries for both of us, if you care to cook. Failing that, I could have breakfast ready when you arrive, or we could even make breakfast together. I can be totally flexible. Which would you prefer my dear?"

Sara did not at all like the direction this discussion was going. Nor did she appreciate being called his "dear." She fully intended their relationship to remain professional. In her mind making breakfast together, or even sharing breakfast together, crossed boundaries inappropriately.

"Thanks Jack, for your graciousness," she heard herself responding. "But I would really prefer to have breakfast with Corrie, before I come." Then she hastily and defensively continued, "You know how difficult teenagers can be, so it is very important for us to stay connected. Taking time each morning to share our plans for the day really helps us communicate and stay in touch with each other. You do understand, don't you?" she finished rather lamely.

An obvious look of disappointment flashed across his handsome features, almost immediately replaced by the polished look and tone of business.

"Of course. That will be just fine, "he said somewhat stiffly. "I will endeavor to have my morning routine complete by the time you arrive. From time to time, however, I may need to involve you in some, shall we say, domestic duties. Like preparing and serving coffee, and perhaps a little delicacy, when I am meeting with clients or local business associate drop by. Would that be acceptable, Mrs. Hill?"

At least he had stopped with the 'my dear,' Sara thought, but now things seemed a little too stiff in the opposite direction. "Well, I suppose that would be a normal part of a receptionist's duties . . ."

"Excellent!" Jack again interrupted. "Now as to compensation, I plan on paying you every two weeks, based on a salary of $200 per month. Thus your first paycheck will be $100, paid to you in two weeks, all things being equal." Before she could even respond or think about negotiating, he had jumped to his feet. "Now then, let's get to work, shall we?"

Somewhat in a daze, Sara followed him from the porch to a cluttered, decidedly untidy office. And so began her day and her week of sorting, cleaning, filing and packing all types of papers, from legal documents to advertising brochures offering attractive parcels of land for sale.

Each day began with coffee and planning in the "on display room," as Sara came to think of it. It seemed as if Mrs. Talkaday, or some other neighbor, passed by each and every day, just at that meeting time. Why did Jack insist on continuing this silly routine?

The schedule than proceeded with filing, sorting, going out for more boxes and the somewhat welcome interruptions of local businessmen arriving for coffee. Sara had met most of them when searching for a job so they joked with her about making a better cup of coffee than Jack did. Certainly the cookies she served were a great addition. But they also seemed to convey some uneasiness to her, about her always being there in Jack's home, whenever they showed up during the day.

It was hard for Sara to interpret just exactly what disturbed them, and her self, if she took the time to think about it. But, she was just doing her job, no matter what others thought or speculated. She had to earn a living, didn't she? At least now that a routine had been established, even Corrie had resigned herself to the new arrangement. While there had been a few other awkward moments, working so closely with Jack in his home, Sara had survived, seemingly unscathed. Only once more in the first two weeks had she again needed to make breakfast for a late rising Jack. Now the first payday loomed on the horizon and Sara eagerly anticipated where she would spend the $100.

Chapter 16
Justyn's Story

The livestock shed was nearing completion. Hoping to hear how her first week of work went, Justyn was keenly disappointed that second Saturday morning when only Corrie joined him for the project.

"Mom had to go into town to run some errands for Jack, as well as to do some of her own. They may even make a trip to Grande Prairie for office supplies, so I guess you and me are it for today."

Nodding, Justyn forced himself not to make a disparaging comment about Jack in Corrie's presence.

"Guess we will need to stick together than. Lets use your small Ford tractor and wagon today. We can cut enough rails to make a load, then haul them to the shed and do some more building. Think you can keep up to me on the other end of that saw?"

"Just watch me!" came a mischievous instant response.

And so they had worked well together, cutting more trees, Corrie clearing and piling brush Justyn limbed from the trees, together loading the wagon, Corrie driving the tractor with Justyn precariously perched on the load to keep it, and himself, from tumbling off. Soon the walls were raised to a full six feet. This height would allow for the winter build-up of straw and manure, without putting the animals through the roof.

A framework for the roof would need to be built next, using some bigger logs again, laid crossways to span the 12' width of the cattle shed. Justyn would need extra muscle for this task so planned to solicit help from another neighbor, Mr. Brown, for the following Saturday.

Care would need to be taken to set at least two rails upright in the twelve foot open side, to help support the front roof beam. It would also need to be about two feet higher than the back beam, the two middle beams at appropriate heights to make a base for the slanted roof. Four to five inch thick rails would then be laid on the support beams to form the roof. These would be nailed to the four support beams. If needed, old boards could be used to cover any gaps between logs and then a layer of straw bales could be added for insulation, to keep the snow cover from melting down through the roof and onto the warm animals.

Still highly motivated, Corrie proved herself a worthy worker. Quick to learn, she became adept at being at the right place at the right time, to steady a rail that Justyn was shaping to fit snug or to scamper out of the way as a tree they had cut began to fall. Somehow she also managed to maintain a steady stream of conversation, mostly about school or community events. Justyn rather enjoyed her dialog, or rather, listening to her monologue. He only became uncomfortable when she tried to draw him out. Two areas of discussion that he specifically avoided were speaking about Jack and answering any probing questions about his own past.

As to the first topic, Sara working for Jack, Justyn still felt clearly irritated, if not down right angry, though he could not clearly say why. Best to just leave that topic alone. Besides, the arrangement seemed to be working out okay. At least from what Corrie shared, Sara was busy but unharmed, though Justyn had bristled when Corrie mentioned Sara making breakfast for a sleepy headed Jack. In any case, Justyn would feel a whole lot better when the office moved from the private home to the public spot on Main street. Adding to his agitation was his having overheard the beginnings of what could become an unpleasant rumor. He had been at the post office lobby, digging his mail out from his box, when he overheard Mrs. Talkaday mention something about that Hill woman being over to the realtor's house early every morning.

"Wouldn't be surprised but that she spends the night too!" had been her assessment.

Slamming his metal mailbox door closed with a little more force than necessary, Justyn had strode from the lobby without looking at anyone. Though he knew Sara was totally innocent, others did not and it didn't seem common knowledge yet that a new reality office was opening in town. Something about this whole thing just did not sit well with Justyn. Thus it would be a tremendous relief when the office was moved into the public eye.

As to the second issue, his own past, Justyn preferred not to think about it himself, never mind discuss it with an impressionable teenager.

He had grown up near the town of Peace River, some 90 miles north and west from where he now lived. Though his parents had taken him to church throughout his childhood, he had chosen to rebel in his teen years. When his parents disciplined him for "sowing wild oats," he had decided to leave home and move to the big city, the oil money rich and booming Edmonton, capital of Alberta. He had been on his own ever since, working on odd jobs at first in the city, then out on the oil patch. The oil rigs paid good money, offered lots of hours and they also provided housing and food. It wasn't long before Justyn's lifestyle had turned around and picked up pace. His money bought him a spot in a high living, 'devil may care' group of youth who hung out together. It was in that group that he had met Jane Anne. At first they had just hung out in the same group, but as a mutual attraction developed, they spent more and more time together as a couple within the group. After a few drinks they would both loosen up and enjoy each other's company.

But just when Justyn thought they were ready to make some type of commitment to each other, she dumped him and ran off with another guy. They had moved to Calgary and the rumor came back that she was pregnant. Justyn never saw, or heard from, Jane Anne again. That had been fifteen years ago.

As a result of that experience, Justyn had vowed never to trust his heart to another woman. It just hurt too much. This bitter experience had also served to keep him one step removed from trusting God. Justyn had wanted to run his own life and not let anyone share in that control.

Having lost the joy of his high flying crowd, Justyn chose to loose himself in the oil patch, working seven days a week, ten hours a day. His goal now was to make enough money to buy a horse ranch, where he could hide away from people and live in peace. In time the money had come. So had the ranch, but not the peace he had anticipated. From his religious upbringing Justyn knew that true peace could only come from God. Thus, over the years, he had gradually reopened his heart to God, but he was not yet ready to fully hand over the reins of his life. He would cautiously continue to feel his way in that relationship, as well as any other that came his way.

And so, whenever Corrie began to probe his past with her endless questions, Justyn would steer the conversation in a different direction. At one point he had even needed to become somewhat angry at her persistence in trying to draw him out. That anger had finally silenced her and they had finished the day's task in reasonably companionable silence.

After a light lunch with Corrie, Justyn had headed back home to check on his horses and do some needed hoof trimming on two of them. As he tackled this strenuous task by himself, he couldn't help but feel the aloneness around him. Even Corrie's chatter was preferable to this emptiness. The disappointment he felt for having missed visiting with Sara also keenly resurfaced. What was the matter with him anyhow, mooning over something that didn't exist?

The horse whose hoof he was trimming stamped her foot, knocking the shears aside. Realizing he had almost cut into the quick of her hoof, he decided to concentrate on the task at hand, before he did some real damage. He needed to keep his wits about him to run a horse ranch. Besides, he was too old to start running off half cocked, losing his head and his heart to a pretty face. She was pretty; he had to say that for her. But was there any potential for a relationship? Best to just be a good neighbor and leave things take care of themselves. That way trust could build slowly, over time, if it built at all.

Chapter 17
Keeping Pigs Happy

The Fall routine of school and chores kept Corrie quite busy. "Don't know why they dump all this homework on us all the time. Half of this stuff I will never use anyway, so what is the point?!" she exclaimed, exasperation in her voice.

Sara would quietly take the time to listen to her complaints and gently encourage her to finish each task. And so the assignments would get done and Corrie would be free to slip outside to enjoy the Fall air, revel in the colorful leaves and crunch through the piles of fallen ones, crisp under her feet.

Her favorite task had become the livestock shed. Whether it was because it had been her idea, or because she was able to work with Uncle Justyn at it, she didn't stop to figure out. But Saturdays were her favorite day, her excitement waking her up at dawn, though normally she had to drag herself, sometimes with help, out of bed each school morning.

Corrie enjoyed her interaction with Justyn. He was such a good listener, even if he didn't like to talk much about his past. They also seemed to come up with good ideas together.

Like last Saturday it struck her that the two remaining pigs may not cooperate in living with the cow and two horses in the same shed, given their constant need to root around, even if it was the bedding for the other animals. And then what about when there were little piglets? Wouldn't they be in danger of getting trampled by the larger animals?

In discussing this dilemma with Justyn, he had come up with the idea of fashioning a rail gate across one of the back corners of the building. The pigs could then be restricted to this triangular space, keeping them separate from the rest of the livestock. Once piglets arrived on the scene, the lower part of the gate could be blocked in with strips of plywood, to keep them from crawling out of their safe place. Yet by being in the same building, all the animals would still benefit from one another's body heat.

"But will they be happy is such a small place?" she had asked, referring to the little triangle behind the gate. The thought of keeping pigs happy had almost caused Justyn to burst out laughing, but with supreme effort he contained himself, as he looked into the extremely serious eyes of the teenager before him.

"In winter, when it is cold, they will be happy to be in a warm space, no matter how small. As long as you remember to feed them there, they will be, ah, happy. We could also salvage some boards from the burnt barn and build a wooden fence out from the shed. Then you could let them into that penned area on warm days, to exercise and root around."

Even though it would mean another Saturday's work for Justyn, Corrie had been jubilant about the idea and so the plan had been set.

The only small cloud on the nearer horizon was that Justyn had made Corrie promise to stay clear when he and the neighbor hoisted the hefty roof beams into place the next Saturday, using the front end loader of his tractor.

"Placing those swaying timbers will be tricky enough without me having to watch out for dropping one on you" Justyn had admonished. Well, she would keep a discreet distance, at least until what she perceived as the tricky part was done.

Chapter 18
Payday

Sara had looked forward all week to Friday. Not only were things very nearly ready to move the office to Main street, but Friday would be her first payday. Even Jack sensed her excitement as the day neared, thought he misinterpreted it to mean she really enjoying working for, and with, him. As a result, he too became more jovial as the week wore on, not to mention even a little forward at times.

Towards the end of the week, however, Jack's mood changed markedly. He became somewhat irritable, brooding over something he refused to talk about.

"Jack, am I doing something wrong? Have I angered you in some way?" Sara finally demanded on Thursday, unable to stand the ambiance any longer.

At this outburst Jack actually smiled. "No, my dear, you are not doing anything wrong. In fact, you are the best thing that has happened to me in a long time."

He approached her then and solicitously took her hand. They were in the glassed in porch for their regular morning coffee and planning chat.

"I am just having some business problems. That's all. Things in land sales are not moving as fast as I had hoped." Looking deep into her eyes, he continued, "But there is nothing to worry your pretty little head about. You just keep encouraging me with that buoyant spirit and gracious smile of yours. Together we make quite a great team."

He patted her hand gently, looked for a moment like he wanted to lean over and kiss her, then obviously thought better of it and left to prepare some papers for a meeting.

Catching her breath and trying to still her pounding heart from the sensuous encounter that almost was, Sara began to busy herself as well. Jack was gone for the rest of the day, leaving Sara to ponder the potential of their relationship. "What would it be like to be kissed by Jack?" She quickly banished the unbidden thought from her mind, at least for the time being, and tried to focus on what might be amiss with the business and how it might affect her new job.

By two o'clock she ran out of office work to do so chose to tidy up the office area, the living room and finally, the kitchen. However, she absolutely refused to set foot anywhere near Jack's bedroom, though it probably needed tidying as well. Now was not the time to enter that space, though perhaps down the road--Sara cut off this train of thought and forced herself to finish her last task. Since Jack had not returned by the end of her workday, she locked up the house and headed home, unsure what to think of Jack's recent moodiness and today's unusual absence. Well, she did have much more important things to think about, she reminded herself. "Rather than musing over Jack's possible troubles, I need to think about how I will spend my first paycheck" she reasoned.

"Groceries would be first," her musing continued, "including buying some special things, like white sugar and refined flour. They had not had either for some time. Fresh eggs and bacon would be a welcome change from oatmeal every morning. And then raisins for the oatmeal would brighten the rest of the mornings as well. Then there was fabric to make new dresses, something she and

Corrie both needed desperately. Corrie's school dress was looking a little shabby and outgrown, while Sara's," she just shook her head, "well after all she was now a business women. She would need to look sharp once they were past the packing and unpacking stage and opened for business in the new office down town.

"Then there were nails for the livestock shed roof, hay to see the cow and horses through the winter (what little she had left from last year, she reminded herself, had been burned in the loft when the barn went), and grain for the stock and the pigs . . . well, the dream could just go on and on."

As Sara pulled into the lane at home, she had to force herself to stop dreaming. They still needed so much, but how far would a paycheck of $100 go? And, she dare not spend it all at once. Rather, she must dole it out carefully and frugally, or it would disappear like a drop of milk in the bucket at milking time.

Upon popping into the house to say Hi to Corrie, she was reminded that it was her turn to milk. Finding the cow in the pasture, she urged her into the corral and tied her to a fence post. Fetching a milk pail from the porch, and her stool from outside the corral gate, Sara began the task of stripping the cow's udder. As the warm milk frothed in the clean pail, she again thanked God for fresh milk and a tame milk cow.

Corrie had supper ready when Sara returned from doing chores. Over eating and cleaning up afterwards, they had a lively chat, trying to prioritize their greatest needs and where tomorrow's income would be best spent. The evening ended with a review of Corrie's homework and then the reading of a Scripture passage together. Why they continued this particular family ritual, neither woman knew, but they both continued to enjoy the sense of peace and wellbeing it seemed to give them. The part of the reading that stuck with them tonight was, "Trust in the Lord, and do good: so shalt thou dwell in the land, and verily thou shalt be fed. Delight thyself also in the Lord; and he will give thee the desires of thine heart. Commit thy way unto the Lord; trust also in him, and he shall bring it to pass" (Psalm 37:3-5). God had provided for them to be fed. God had made a way for them to stay on their own land. All they needed to do now was to keep trusting in him. Between the encouragement of Scripture and the assurance of income the next day, both Corrie and Sara slept soundly that night.

Sara was completely unprepared for what transpired the next morning. Arriving precisely at 8:00 am Friday morning, she knocked crisply on Jack's door. Even though she had a key, she always preferred to knock when Jack was home. She definitely did not want to embarrass either of them by bursting in on him when he might be indisposed.

When no one answered, she knocked again, a little more loudly. Beginning to think that he had not returned from being away the day before, she began searching in her purse for the key. Suddenly the door creaked open a sliver and Jack's rumpled head appeared, barely visible.

"I'm very sorry, my dear, but I won't be needing your services today. I arrived back too late last evening to tell you. Take the time off in lieu of having worked last Saturday. We will straighten things out on Monday."

With that comment complete, the door began to close. Stunned, Sara managed to sputter out, just before the door clicked shut, "But Jack, it's payday. I thought . .

." she was unable to continue, tears threatening the corners of her eyes. The door opened slightly once more.

"Yes dear, we will need to discuss that on Monday as well. Come around 10:00 am instead of this early." The stern response brooked no further discussion.

The door closed with finality, leaving Sara standing there holding her key, which she had just found and now no longer needed. Stumbling back to her pickup with tears clouding her eyes, she didn't even notice Mrs. Talkaday going by on her daily walk, muttering something about what the world was coming to, given the loose morals of some people, even grown women who should know better.

Chapter 19
More Important Than Money

Still dazed as she drove through town, Sara tried to think if there was anything she needed while here, so the trip would not be totally wasted. But even when she forced her mind to focus on their needs, it immediately swung back to the fact that she had no money to pay for any purchases. Tears of disappointment, and even anger, continued to pour down her cheeks and so she headed home, not wanting to face anyone just now.

By the time she reached her lane, she had calmed herself somewhat and was trying to rationalize what had just happened that made her feel so devastated. "Its only a temporary setback," she tried to tell herself. "On Monday I'll have my paycheck and everything will be fine. I'm not a child. I can delay gratification for a few days," she whispered to herself, trying to sound convincing. But something about the look in Jack's eye, the one peeking out the door, and the abruptness of being given the day off totally unexpectedly, continued to haunt her as she began working on some of the tasks around the house that had been let slide since she started her job.

The day passed incredibly slowly and Sara was almost elated to hear the familiar rumble of the school bus stopping at the end of the driveway. At least now she would have someone to talk too, even if she needed to be careful with how much of her fear she shared with Corrie.

"Wow, you are home early Mom! Already celebrating your first payday?" Corrie bubbled as she entered the kitchen. Seeing no evidence of packages, she babbled on, "Did you come home first so I could join you on a shopping spree?" Finally Corrie noticed her

Mother's subdued manner and stopped short. "What?" she demanded. She searched her mother's face, this time waiting for an answer.

"I didn't get paid today Corrie. Jack is having some business problems and so he gave me the day off instead. He said we will work out the pay on Monday." Sara did her best to suppress the tears that threatened to resurface and to make her voice sound more confident than she really felt.

"That dirty cheat still will pay you, won't he?" Corrie replied caustically, cutting right through to the core, as teenagers are prone to do.

"I hope so Corrie. I really do." Sara could no longer hold Corrie's gaze. "But you shouldn't speak so disrespectfully of your elders."

"Elders, nothing. As to respect, what I said is mild compared to the stories going around school about him and . . ." Corrie suddenly broke off. Hanging up her coat and putting her books away, she was glad her mother's preoccupation had caused her to miss what Corrie had almost said.

Trying to cheer her Mom up, Corrie decided to switch to something more positive.

"Well, at least you have tomorrow off so you can help Uncle Justyn, Mr. Brown and myself put the roof on the livestock shed. The walls are all up and they will use Justyn's tractor to lift the big beams in place. Then we just need to nail on the rails . . ." her mother had suddenly blanched!

"Now what Mom?"

"The nails! I was planning to buy the nails for that project today, with my paycheck, and now I can't.

What will we do?" she wailed, slumping onto the couch in a heap, her face buried in her hands.

"Maybe Uncle Justyn has some he could bring, or Mr. Brown. We could replace them when you do get paid on Monday," Corrie enthused hopefully, not able to stand seeing her mother so distraught.

"I hate to even ask" Sara's muffled and despondent reply filtered through her fingers, still covering her face. "They are already providing all the labor free of charge, and Mrs. Brown is even helping with a lunch."

Suddenly another idea struck Corrie. "I know!" she burst out. "We can gather nails from the burn site of the barn. And we can pull others from the scrap heap of partially burnt boards. Surely we can find enough to keep the project going ahead."

A smile actually broke through the flushed face and Sara bounded up to give Corrie a big hug. "I really appreciate you and your 'never say quit' spirit. That is an excellent idea. Let's go right now and get started, so we can use what daylight is left. When it gets darker, we'll haul a load of boards with nails in, over under the yard light and then we can pull them after supper. Let's get changed into our grubbies and get to work. Grab a cinnamon roll on the way out, to tide you over because supper will be late. I'll round up some buckets for the nails we collect, two hammers and a goose neck to pry out the stubborn nails." Her voice was tinged with excitement now too.

By late that night an interesting assortment of nails had been collected. The women had even tied to pound straight the bent ones, in an effort to salvage all they could. Hopefully the crew arriving in the morning would not be too fussy to utilize the used nails.

The next day dawned bright and clear, though a little on the cool side for an October morning. Sara and Corrie hurried through chores and a light breakfast. They were just finishing when they heard the rumble of Justyn's tractor. Glancing out they noticed a pickup following it. The crew was arriving.

Everyone immediately set to work, excited to have the project underway. Though Justyn originally had wanted Corrie to stay clear when the roof beams were set, it soon became apparent that extra hands were needed to guide the swinging logs into place. With Justyn working the fork lift to raise the chain attached beam to the right height, and Mr. Brown catching and securing one end, it fell to Sara and Corrie to guide the other end in place and secure it. Though Sara dropped one nail and sent another flying with a miss hit with the hammer, she did manage to secure each of her beam ends, while Corrie held them in place, both women doing their best to stay astride the six foot rail wall, hanging on with their legs to free their hands for the work.

Starting first at the back of the shed, to accommodate the loader and the swinging logs, the team worked persistently until all four of the roof beams were in place. Once both ends of the highest log, the one over the front opening of the shed, was secured, Mr. Brown shinnied along it to where the two upright posts had been dug into the ground. He then nailed the log to these upright posts, which would provide extra support for the open side of the shed. Once the entire structure was secured, he stepped into the loader and was safely lowered to the ground.

Letting out the breath that they hadn't realized they were holding while Mr. Brown dangled on the beam, Mother and Daughter cheered and clapped. Everyone was safe and the essential structure was complete.

Next the crew worked in two's to load rails onto the bucket of the front-end loader. All the rails had to be long enough to run the full length of the shed and a few shorter ones would be needed to fill in the wall gaps produced by the slanted roof. With a dozen rails somewhat precariously balanced on the bucket of the loader, Justyn carefully maneuvered the tractor around to the back of the shed. From this lowest point they could be more easily slid up the slanting roof and into place.

As this task began, it again became evident that all hands were needed. This time Justyn balanced on the uppermost beam, attaching the end of the rails, while Mr. Brown moved back and forth to attach the rails to the second and third beam. This left the fourth beam for Sara to deal with, something that was a little tricky since the rails varied in length and the overhang somewhat obscured where the last roof beam was. The overhangs could be left, or cut off later, after all where attached. With everyone else busy, Corrie too had a job. She carefully stood on the back wall and pulled an end of each rail up onto the roof from the loader, and slid it up to those doing the nailing.

The system worked well and soon nearly all the rails from the first load were in place. So far no one had even complained about the used nails and they seemed to be working quite well, even though a few had to be straightened several times. The only near catastrophe was when Corrie accidentally knocked the last rail off the bucket as she was wrestling the second to the last one onto the roof. Fortunately the tumbling rail fell away without striking Sara, who was closest to it, and without smashing into the tractor itself. The fear injected by the mishap was quickly released with jesting and jabs at Corrie about trying to shorten the job and intending to wreck Justyn's tractor. In a jovial mode now, the crew climbed down from the roof and went to put a second load of rails on the loader. This task complete, but before they could resume building the roof, Mrs. Brown summoned them to lunch.

Sara had been somewhat concerned about being able to provide enough food for a hard working crew. It was much to her delight and relief then when, earlier in the week, Mrs. Brown had offered to provide a good portion of the meal and set it up for the crew while they labored at the construction site. Now all was in readiness, set up on the picnic table in the back yard. As the workers lined up at the pump to wash, taking turns to pump water for each other, the aroma of fried chicken and fresh bread tantalized them.

"There is nothing like hard work and fresh, cool air to bring out the appetite," Mr. Brown commented. A capable cook, his wife had provided amply for even this hungry crew, and all were well fed by the time each eater had groaned to a halt.

After such a hearty meal, it was with some difficulty that the crew dragged themselves back to work on the shed. The second load of logs seemed to take longer to use up than the first one had in the morning shift, and the third load took forever, but finally the task was done. The roof was fully covered by rails, and where gaps had occurred, used boards had been nailed in place. Now all that was left was to add straw bales to break the wind and seal out any moisture that might drip through from melting snow.

With numb hands from all the pounding, and weary muscles from all the extraordinary motions that she wasn't used to, Sara stumbled up the porch steps and into the house, having waved goodbye to her wonderful neighbors. Since Corrie had a little more energy left than she did, Sara sent her to bring in water to be heated on the stove for a bath. "Nothing like a good soak to ease tired muscles," she sighed.

Suddenly it hit Sara that not once all day had she worried about her job situation. Somehow, being with people who really cared had a way of easing life's burdens.

"I guess there still are things more important than money" she mumbled to herself as she climbed into bed that night, feeling rich for having just experienced a few of those very things. Little did she know that she was about to learn just how precious "more important than money" really was.

Chapter 20
Appearance of Evil

At church the next morning the Browns, Hills and Justyn exchanged especially hardy greetings, teasing one another about sore muscles and joking about hiring themselves out as an expert, experienced construction crew.

While this interaction was particularly warm, Sara couldn't help but sense that her reception by several other ladies in the church was quite cool, if not downright frozen. Trying to shrug it off as overactive imagination, Sara was nevertheless troubled in spirit as she took her seat beside Corrie in the third pew from the back.

"Am I missing something?" she mused during the silent preparation time before worship began. "And what was that comment Corrie had started to make the other day about stories at school?" Further speculation was interrupted by standing for the first hymn, but Sara was only able to force her brooding thoughts aside by determining to question Corrie further about this issue on the way home from church.

As the congregation turned to greet one another, following the hymn, Sara again felt a slight coolness from those around her. People didn't exactly ignore her but no one went out of their way to come over and greet her either. It was almost as if people were avoiding her. In looking around, Sara also noticed that Jack was, at least to her, conspicuously absent. This sudden realization catapulted her anxiety back into the foreground, causing her to miss the next part of the service entirely. She reconnected with her surroundings only when she heard

Pastor Alden introduce, and begin reading, his Bible text
for the day.

"Wherefore lay apart all filthiness and superfluity
of naughtiness, and receive with meekness the engrafted
work, which is able to save your souls. But be ye doers of
the word, and not hearers only, deceiving your own
selves. For if any be a hearer of the word, and not a doer,
he is like unto a man beholding his natural face in a glass:
For he beholdeth himself, and goeth his way, and
straightway forgetteth what manner of man he was. But
whoso looketh into the perfect law of liberty, and
continueth therein, he being not a forgetful hearer, but a
doer of the word, this man shall be blessed in his deed. If
any man among you seem to be religious, and bridleth not
his tongue, but deceiveth his own heart, this man's
religion is vain. Pure religion and undefiled before God
and the Father is this. To visit the fatherless and widows
in their affliction, and to keep himself unspotted from the
world" (James 1:21-27 KJV).

"Now what does it mean to keep oneself
unspotted, or unstained, by the world?" Pastor Alden
asked as he launched into his message. "What things in
this world have this ability to contaminate us? I'm sure
we could all quickly identify major sins in our
community, like stealing someone else's cattle and re-
branding them to our own symbol, or cheating someone
out of money or other valuable possessions that rightly
belong to them. Indeed, these things are very wrong and
should not be named among us as Christians. But what
about relationships? If a certain relationship causes us to
compromise our Christian convictions and we begin
living like the world, is not this also wickedness that
stains us and that our text asks us to put aside?"

Everyone was listening intently now and Sara noticed a few quick glances in her direction.

"The picture James uses here is of soiling our garments. Now we all know what the gumbo clay around here can do to our clothes. Those stains are very obvious. But other stains may begin much more subtly. For example, perhaps at first we do not even notice that anything is amiss with our outfit. Perhaps something we were eating dropped unnoticed onto our shirt or blouse. It remains there until, quite by accident we notice it, or someone else brings it to our attention. Perhaps by then the stain has begun to set but we think, 'no big deal. I'll just wash it out when I get home.' But the longer the stain remains on the cloth, the more difficult it will be to remove. Immediate, appropriate action is needed or the garment could be stained permanently.

The stains of this world that tend to destroy us are the ones that sneak up on us subtly, like this. Satan loves to use worldly temptations to stain our lives, and he is a master at keeping them hidden until the long-term damage is done. Let us not be drawn in by his trickery! Let us not be fooled by what appears in the world's eyes as insignificant stains that will easily wash out. God commanded that we flee even the appearance of evil. May we take to heart Christ's warning! May we cast out sin, whether evil actions or unhealthy relationships, the moment they are brought to our attention! Then we will be doers of the word and not hearers only, as our text describes. My prayer for each of you is that you will be doers of the word, and not hearers only, and thereby you will be able to avoid being stained by the world."

From where he sat in the back pew, Justyn had to admit it was a very thought provoking sermon. And he had to agree with the Pastor. It certainly was easy to let down one's guard and allow principles and practices of the world to creep in and contaminate the Christian lifestyle. Things like thinking we deserve to be given all the comforts of life, like the rich people enjoy. Behaviors like tromping on someone else if it gets us further ahead. Or dropping loyalty to a Christian brother or sister at the first sign of problems, either perceived or real.

It was this latter point that stuck, just like a burr to the socks of someone walking through weeds, irritating Justyn to no end. He too had noticed the rather cool reception Sara was receiving from some of the church folk. He too, from his vantage point at the back, had noticed the glances her way as the Pastor spoke of wickedness and the appearance of evil. With each glance he became more furious and it was all he could do to keep from jumping up and calling them all hypocrites. How could these so-called Christian brothers and sisters turn their back on Sara so quickly, based only on malicious rumors? Why couldn't they love her enough to go and talk with her about what they were hearing and thereby uncover the truth?

"You are looking mighty serious and even stern today, Justyn."

It was Pastor Alden. Unnoticed, Justyn had reached him in the handshake line as everyone was filing out of church.

"Fine sermon, Pastor" he quickly rebounded to the present. "We all needed to hear it." He purposely stressed the "all" loudly enough for those around him to hear, "and we probably need to hear more about healthy relationships, how to strengthen one another to beat Satan at his subtle game." Now Justyn was preaching as he firmly shook the Pastor's hand.

"A good idea Justyn. Very good indeed! I will give your advice some serious thought for upcoming sermons."

A little embarrassed by the limelight, Justyn hurried outside and was just in time to overhear Corrie ask Sara if she could join the youth group for a picnic.

"They have lots of food and want me to come along" Corrie enthused.

Hesitating only for a moment, Sara responded, "Okay, but give me a call if you need a ride home after." Secretly she was glad Corrie was choosing to spend some time with her peers. They seemed to do that less and less frequently. Sara had almost begun to worry about it. Now she was relieved, as she watched Corrie dart off to the giggling girls waiting for her.

"Sounds like a right good idea" Justyn spoke at her elbow, somewhat surprising even himself. "Not too many nice Fall days like this left to enjoy. We could make up some sandwiches at my house and go for a horseback ride and picnic ourselves if you like." He spoke the words rather hastily in his nervousness, as he walked with Sara towards her truck and out of earshot of the others leaving church.

Stopping at her truck door, Sara responded, a thoughtful look on her face. "Actually that does sound like fun. I don't think I have really ridden horseback since the fire. Both my horse and I need the outing. How about if I run home and change, find something to go with your sandwiches, and then meet you down by the creek that runs between our places?"

"Sounds good to me" Justyn agreed, finding himself more enthusiastic than he had been in quite some time. Helping her close her pickup door after she climbed in, Justyn added, "Meet you at that big bend in the creek in about half an hour."

It was actually a full 45 minutes before the lovely brunette and her horse loped into view. Having arrived at the designated spot in twenty-five minutes, Justyn had begun to think he had miss communicated the location of the rendezvous. Thus he was very happy to hear the rhythmic beat of a lopping horse over the crackle of the small fire he had built. But he wasn't quite prepared for the breathtaking site as horse and rider broke through the tree line and came into full view. Sara had tied back her long hair with a red bandana, causing it to stream out behind her as she rode. Justyn also noticed the practiced ease with which she sat her horse, the oneness she showed with the animal she rode. She was riding bareback! "Of course," Justyn began to scold himself, "she lost the saddle in the fire. Why didn't I think to loan her one?" But the personal chastisement had only a moment to linger. As Sara drew up, he noticed the blue-checkered top and matching blue jeans that he just knew would accentuate her blue eyes.

Slipping off the rounded back of her mount as nimble as a youngster, Sara tied her horse near Justyn's and came over to join him by the crackling fire, just hot enough now to lightly toast sandwiches held over it on green, forked willow branches. In awe of her natural beauty, which was heightened by being stress free for the moment, Justyn felt tongue tied and awkward as to how to greet her. He resorted to teasing as a way out.

"I see you remember how to ride. And even without a saddle. I'm amazed that old nag of yours could run this far."

"That 'old nag' has plenty of energy left for me, especially riding with no saddle horn to hang on to" Sara responded happily, refusing to rise to the bait and spoil the exhilarating ride she had just taken. "I always did like this picturesque little glen in the creek bed. It's so pretty. It must be on my property, don't you think?" Now her eyes were sparkling mischievously.

With superhuman effort Justyn resisted the urge to simply scoop her up, light five foot seven frame and all and just tickle her until she cried "Uncle."

Instead he calmly responded in soft words he hoped could be heard over the pounding of his heart, "Why don't I toast you a sandwich while you pour the coffee from that thermos over there. Then we can sit on that log and enjoy <u>our</u> scenic spot."

Catching the little word "our," Sara giggled as she un-slung a little shoulder bag and opened it. She pulled out two cups for the coffee, since she for one really didn't want to share only the thermos cup, two apples and two cinnamon buns. Finishing arranging them on a towel she had brought for that purpose, placed on a stump nearby, she received her warmed sandwich, and poured the coffee while Justyn toasted his own sandwich. Seating her self comfortably on the designated log, she let out a large, contented sigh.

"Oh why couldn't life always be this peaceful? Life is just so much more precious when we are content with the little joys it offers."

"Isn't that the truth" Justyn grunted as he came and lowered himself onto the log, at what he hoped was a comfortable distance from this enchanting woman.

After sitting in companionable silence for a few moments, munching on their sandwiches, Sara suddenly burst out, "Justyn, we have an honest friendship, don't we?"

Not sure of where this statement was leading, and if he wanted it to be more than that, Justyn somewhat hesitantly grunted in the affirmative, having just stuffed the last piece of his sandwich into his mouth.

"What I mean is," Sara continued, looking off into the distance, "if I ask you a question straight out, you would tell me the truth, wouldn't you, even if it was not what I wanted to hear?"

Trying to appear calm on the outside, Justyn's mind and heart began to have a race with each other. Was she going to ask him to declare his feelings for her? Did he even know himself how he felt about her?

"I would sure try" he managed to squeeze out as he now suddenly became interested in starring at a spot far down the creek.

"Well, around town lately and now today in church, I have felt like I am being shut out by people, even ones I thought were my friends. Do you have any idea what is going on? Am I just imagining things? Please tell me the truth" she implored.

Now she looked at him expectantly, her blue eyes large and penetrating, conveying trust and a touch of fear. Yet despite the mixed emotion written there, her pretty face also conveyed a determination to know the real truth.

Finding some difficulty in swallowing the last bite of his suddenly very dry pastry, Justyn took a long swig of coffee, both to buy time and to still his edgy nerves. This was not at all what he had expected. Of all the times, this was the least best time to bring up this topic. How much should he say? Would it ruin the preciousness of the moments they were now sharing? The truth was very stark. Would it help her to know what the gossips were saying, or would it only hurt her. When he did finally turn to meet her expectant, honest gaze, he knew he had to tell at least as much as he had heard.

"Well Sara" there was a remarkable gentleness to his tone that Sara had not heard before, "Valleyview is a small town and everybody speaks to everyone else about anything that they see and hear. Unfortunately, truth gets mixed up with gossip by the time a story makes its rounds and soon it's hard to separate out the actual facts."

His mouth still dry, he quickly swallowed another mouthful of coffee while Sara looked like she had stopped breathing, she was listening so intently, apprehension beginning to drive the serenity from her face.

"You mean there is gossip floating around about me?" she beseeched breathlessly, so quiet even Justyn's keen ears had difficulty picking it up. "And just what have people found to discuss about me?"

Becoming increasingly uncomfortable by the moment, Justyn didn't know whether to put his arm around this vulnerable, sweet smelling woman or make a break for his horse and gallop off to safety.

Her eyes again froze him to the spot, unable to flee, unable to retract or stem the conversation now set in motion.

Taking a deep breath, he forced himself to continue. "It seems one of Jack's neighbors has been noticing you over at his house early each morning. She had no idea of the real reason why you were there so has gone ahead and shared some of her own opinions about it." Seeing a fire begin to light in the blue eyes, Justyn hurried on, somewhat defensively, determined to see this gruesome task through. "Seeing you there with Jack, she made some assumptions and, living up to her name, Mrs. Talkaday, she shares what she sees and her interpretation of it, with anyone who will listen. I'm afraid she has even hinted that you spend the nights with Jack too."

The fire spread from her eyes to engulf her voice and her whole body. "Well of all the mean, low down, character assassins I have ever heard," Sara exploded, jumping to her feet. "How could anyone share such trash about me and how could people who know me even listen to it and pass it on?!" Sara never expected an answer. Instead her mind was already racing with how widespread the rumor must be. Certainly the people at church had heard it, and is that what Corrie was hinting at regarding rumors at the High School?

Suddenly the anger drained from her face, to be replaced by a look of near horror as she turned back to face Justyn. All of a sudden, his next answer was the most crucial in the whole world to her.

"Do you believe the rumors, Justyn?" Both her eyes and her voice pleaded that it was not so. "Surely you do not see me as that type of person, do you?"

The look of pain mingled with, was it really love, from those steel gray eyes spoke volumes more than the few words he managed to express. "Sara, I trust you and your integrity completely and always will."

For a moment their eyes held, long enough for the trust to be conveyed, and just when they might have embraced, Sara suddenly scooped up her picnic utensils, thrust them into her carry bag, and strode purposefully to her horse.

Yanking the lines from the tree branch so sharply that it broke in the process, she grabbed the horse's mane and leaped up onto its back. Spinning the horse, she called back to Justyn, "You are a precious friend, Justyn Smith, but if you hang with me, your reputation will be sullied too. I simply won't allow that to happen. We had best go our separate ways, lest we provide the gossips with more ammunition to shoot you down as well."

And with that outburst, given with tears steaming down her face because she truly felt she had just lost her last friend, Sara galloped off across the field in a cloud of dust, unable to hear the protests from the one she had come to care for deeply and felt she had to protect.

As quickly as he could, Justyn extinguished the stubborn fire, gathered his belongings and mounted up, intending to ride after her. Though she was already out of sight, her horse's galloping tracks were plain across the harvested field. Not sure why, Justyn drew in his horse just before galloping out into the open from the trees lining the creek. Looking about, he noticed several cars leisurely driving down the road, no doubt on their Sunday outing. Choosing to retain his cover in the trees, Justyn had to grudgingly agree with at least part of what Sara had said. No sense being seen chasing after her, even if on horseback. Who knows what stories could be made of a rendezvous down by the creek. Best to let them think she was just out on a ride by herself.

But whatever it took, Justyn vowed to the storm that was raging within him as he rode home, he would do everything he could to clear Sara's name or go down with her in infamy, if that was the only other option.

Chapter 21

Trust in the Midst of Pain

Sara ended up riding her horse the long way home. After the initial burst of speed away from the creek, Sara forced them both to slow down because the tears streaming from her eyes severely obscured her vision. But for her sure-footed horse, she could easily have injured them both. Slowing the horse to a walk, she let the tears flow freely, tears for the unfairness, tears for the persecution, tears of now feeling abandoned. She simply poured it all out to the only One she had left, to a loving God who assured her that he still cared. To the One who had said, in the devotional just the other day, "And he shall bring forth they righteousness as the light, and thy judgment as the noonday" (Psalms 37:6). Could she really trust God to do that for her?

Finally the tears ceased and Sara sensed an awesome peace deep within her soul. She didn't know how, but since she had maintained her integrity despite Jack's advances, God would now be faithful to her and bring her through this predicament.

By the time her peace with God was settled, Sara noticed that her faithful horse had managed unaided to steer the way home and so together they covered the last few hundred yards at a light canter. As they entered the yard, Sara noticed that Corrie was home and trying to do something rather hurriedly at the water pump by the house. Quickly using her bandana to dry her eyes and restore some semblance of calm to her face, Sara called a greeting and rode on to the granary, now storage shed, where she stored the few remaining pieces of tack, like her bridle, that had not been in the barn the night of the fire.

As she curried dried sweat from her horse's coat, Corrie came strolling over to join her. Though she had tried to hide it with cold water from the pump, Sara could still tell at a glance that Corrie had also been crying.

Trying not to comment directly, she asked causally, "You're back early. How was the picnic?"

"All right I guess." Corrie refused to meet Sara's gaze. "It got a little boring so I asked them to bring me home."

Obviously trying to change the subject, Corrie declared, "Mom, look at your pants. They are as dirty as this horse. You must have had quite a ride. I didn't know you could ride bareback."

"I learned as a little girl," Sara replied, still brushing the horse. "Some things one just never forgets." They continued on then in companionable silence until the task was complete and the horse was released into the pasture. As mother and daughter watched, the gelding immediately found a dry patch of dirt to lie down on and roll, his own cure for the itchiness on his back caused by sweating.

While Sara smiled at the site, she heard several sniffles from her daughter. Guessing what might be the problem, Sara gently placed her arm around Corrie. Feeling no stiffening or resistance, she pulled her close and whispered in her hair, "I know about the nasty rumors, Corrie, and none of them are true, as you and I both know. People can be so cruel when they start to gossip." Corrie had begun to sob again. "But we have nothing to be ashamed of; we did nothing wrong. Let's carry our heads high and let the truth emerge to set us free."

It was Corrie's turn to release all her pent up emotion, including the fears of having kept dark secrets from the person whom she cared about most, as she clung to her mother and tried to negotiate the porch steps at the same time, through blurred vision. Flopping down on the couch in the living room, in the security of their own house and shielded from hostile ears, Corrie was finally able to unburden what to her were dreadful secrets.

"At school the kids talk about you as if you are the town prostitute." A certain amount of venom appeared in her voice. "They identify Jack as your latest victim and have ideas of who it was before and who it will be after him. They simply have no shame at all, Mother." Corrie was back to sniffling again. "Rubbing it all in my face is their idea of sport. They find it quite hilarious. Even at the church picnic some of the kids started in on me. I never want to be with them again! I hate them, I hate them . . ." her voice trailed off into a fresh burst of tears as the women clung to each other.

Sara had to brush away her own fresh tears as she waited for Corrie's torrent to subside. As it slowed to snuffles and hiccups, she quietly responded, "They are wrong to say such hurtful, hurtful lies. They are allowing Satan to use them and he would like nothing better than to drive you and I away from God and God's church. But do you know what? We are not going to allow Satan to win. In fact, instead of running away, we are going to go to God first, then His church, to work this thing through. It won't be easy, but the truth needs to come out. Will you stand with God and me, through this painful confrontation?" she asked.

She felt her daughter's head nod in the affirmative, though still tightly jammed against her chest.

At least there were the two of them now, fighting as a team and with God on their side. But both would need the peace only God can give, to survive the painful turmoil ahead.

Chapter 22
The Plan

A few more tears were shed the next morning as the two women prepared for sending Corrie off to school. Though she would no doubt be teased some more, Corrie had determined she would ignore it, rather than rising to the bait and reacting each time a comment was purposely flung in her direction.

Sara, on the other hand, had no idea how to prepare for her ten o'clock meeting with Jack. Had he heard the rumors too? Was he concerned? Was there a future to her job, or was she too much bad publicity for a new Reality office about to open? Was that why his business had slowed of late? And what of her paycheck? Would he give it to her today?

It seemed a month had passed, rather than just a weekend, as Sara again pulled her pickup to a stop in front of Jack's house precisely at 10 o'clock. Filled with trepidation, it was with some satisfaction that she could not see Mrs. Talkaday anywhere in sight. Walking up to the door with more confidence then she felt, she took a deep breath and rapped sharply.

Almost immediately the door swung upon, almost on its own volition, to reveal a meticulously groomed Jack, complete with a huge smile on his face.

"Come in, come in my dear. You look lovely today, as always." Taking her by the arm he ushered her in and gently closed the door behind her." Tucking her arm in his, he led her toward the sun porch. "Join me for coffee in our usual spot, won't you?" Not waiting for an answer, he prattled on, "So how are you this fine morning?"

Sara was too stunned to say a single word, incredulous at the dramatic mood change in Jack since last she had seen him. What in the world had transpired to bring about such a reversal?

The small talk continued, mostly on Jack's part, while the coffee was served, by Jack himself no less, and they were comfortably seated in the glassed-in porch. By now Sara's intuitive warning bells were ringing incessantly. What was Jack up to now? He looked like a cat about to pounce on her, the mouse, or at least spring some type of new trap on her. Finally she could stand it no longer.

"Okay Jack. Spill the beans. What is going on?"

"Going on?" Jack exclaimed with mock innocence. "Whatever do you mean my dear?"

"Last I saw you the world had caved in and I wondered if I would still have a job. Now you seem on top of the world and I am treated like royalty. Something positive must have happened in between" she insisted.

"I am hopeful something good is about to happen" Jack purred as he moved to the edge of his seat and again reached for her hand. "The ultimate answer depends upon your decision."

Caught totally by surprise, both by Jack's comment and by his holding her hand, Sara managed to sputter, "How can your well being be dependent on a decision made by me?"

"Well, beautiful lady, I have a proposal, as it were, that should help both you and me out tremendously. Since sales have been slow lately, I find myself in need of a little more collateral to keep my business running. Your farm will fill that bill quite nicely."

Sara jerked up straight at the mention of her farm and almost managed to snatch her hand from Jack's firm grip. But Jack, having anticipated this, held her wrist even more tightly and held up his other hand to silence her pending outburst.

"Now before you respond without giving my proposition careful thought, allow me to tell you what is in the arrangement for you. As you and I both know, you are in need of finances to keep your farm from the taxman. I can help with that. Secondly," he again motioned her to remain silent "and more importantly than merely having a business arrangement, I happen to be aware of your deep desire for me, as is much of the town. Now, in order to save your reputation, as well as that of my future business, I propose that we marry and amalgamate our holdings, as it were." He was purring now. "It's the perfect way out of both of our dilemmas, don't you agree?" He ended on a note of triumph.

Sara had paled considerably. Jack did know about the rumors and was actually using them to force her hand, to actually give him her hand. While she remained speechless, Jack rattled on as convincingly as possible.

"You know our being wed is the most perfect solution, benefiting both of us. I will take care of your financial needs, your personal needs will be met along with mine and the gossipers will run out of fuel for their discussions. My business will benefit with the added collateral of your land and the perceived greater stability of being a married man and we both will enjoy the benefits of marital bliss." The later was mentioned with an openly hungry look in his eye.

Though she tried to keep from showing it, Sara was totally floored by this strange proposal. While the security of marriage appealed to her, as did the assets Jack had to offer, his personal appeal had long since vanished and all she could feel was a sense of being used and manipulated.

"But what of our current arrangement?" She was stalling for time, trying to force her numb mind to come up with a plan. "Once we move into the new office on Main street, business will pick up for you without involving my farm and the regular salary you pay will help me. Won't we both benefit that way too?" she ended rather lamely, even to her ears.

Jack released his strong hold on her hand and stood, towering over her somewhat threateningly for a moment, before going off to stand and stare out the window. Glancing back at her, he finally broke the stilted silence.

"There is not going to be a Reality office on Main Street. Valleyview just does not have the potential to support such an office. Paying rent would further erode my financial base. I would be foolish to proceed in such a direction."

He paused for a brief moment and so Sara jumped in.

"But what of your plans; all the packing; my future job?" Sara implored.

"All non-existent my dear. You have organized and filed my things well enough here that I, or we" he added solicitously, "can operate quite nicely from here. As a team, you could perhaps run this office and I could open one in the larger center of Grande Prairie. As to your pay, it hardly makes sense for me to pay a wage to my wife, or future wife. We would be full partners, pooling our resources and sharing in the profits."

He was again approaching her with that noticeably desirous glint in his eye, so Sara quickly stood and tried to nonchalantly move so that the chair was a protective barrier between them.

"And the $100 you already owe me?" Sara dared to ask, almost holding her breath.

"Owe you for what, my dear? Should I really need to pay you for coming to live at my house during the day as the way to enjoy my company? That would only confirm what some people are saying about your 'profession.' After all, there is no formal job here in my home, only opportunity to become a full partner. Consider your chores here an investment in your future. As to the rumors, perhaps we should just enjoy what you know we both want and lend some credence to what is being said about us anyway."

The ongoing lust in his eyes made very clear the intention he wished to fulfill. Sara found herself beginning to tremble. She had to get herself out of this place, this once tempting situation that had now turned into pure nightmare.

Continuing to keep the chair between them, Sara tried to again stall for time. "I'll need some time to think about your generous proposal and, or course, to discuss it with Corrie. After all she would be part of the family too. Then we would need time to plan the wedding, book the Pastor and the church . . ." her voice trailed off as she ran out of ideas. Until she could physically escape, however, she had to keep stringing Jack along, as if she was genuinely considering his outrageous offer.

"No need for any delay," he smiled gallantly. "I'll simply invite the judge over this afternoon, while he is still in town. As Justice of the Peace, he would fulfill the legal requirements and we could enjoy a husband and wife relationship tonight. What do you say?" He started to come around the chair toward her, one arm reaching for her. "Shall we seal this perfect plan with at least a kiss or whatever else we deem appropriate?" He was almost licking his lips now.

"No!" Sara found herself screaming. Despite her substantial self-control, this was the final straw. She had reached her limit and without even really thinking, she scooped up a large lamp next to the chair and hurled it directly at Jack. Catching him off guard, he warded off the worst of the impact, allowing the lamp to crash to the floor and shatter. The evasive maneuver gave Sara just enough time to bolt past him and out the door, slamming it behind her. Dashing to her pickup, she jumped in and quickly locked both doors. Grabbing her key from her handbag, which she thankfully had grabbed on the way out, she stabbed it into the ignition and turned it. As the engine roared to life, she hastily popped the truck into gear and squealed the tires as she made a hasty exit. Thankfully Jack did not emerge from the house to try and stop her. For a second time within a week, Sara sped through the neighborhood and town, tears streaming down her face, making it hard for her to negotiate her turns and avoid hitting other vehicles.

Chapter 23
True Feelings are Exposed

Jack fumed the entire time it took him to sweep up the fragments from the shattered lamp and restore order to the sun porch. "How could she refuse my generous offer?" he muttered angrily. "I know she has feelings for me. Here I am, offering to share my life and resources with her, and she chooses to throw it in my face and for what, an old run down farm."

But what really was sticking in Jack's craw was that his elaborate plan of manipulation, spread out over an entire month, had actually failed. He had carefully staged things so as to appear the chivalrous knight in shining army, rescuing her from pennilessness and the vicious rumors on her character by the townsfolk. Rumors which he himself had meticulously groomed by making sure that Mrs. Talkaday saw Sara and him together very early every weekday morning.

"Well at least I have ruined her reputation in this community" he consoled himself. "No one else will hire her now. In the end, she will have to come crawling back to me to buy her worthless piece of land, just to pay the taxes. Then she will learn that there is a tremendous cost to turning me down, and I will make sure she pays it to the fullest extent."

Relishing that moment in his mind, he completed cleaning up, put away the broom and garbage, and went to sit at his desk to plot what things would help hasten this latest dream. Perhaps he could let it be known that she was pregnant and that he had done the gallant thing, offering to marry her, but that she had refused. That should help retain his image in the community while further destroying hers. The community would rally to squeeze her out and the farm would soon be his, for little or no cost. Now who could he reliably pass on this latest tidbit of "private information" so that it would spread the quickest?

***

Justyn was at the medical clinic on Main, across from the little theater, having a rather nasty barbwire cut attended to on his right arm. He had been tightening the top wire of his pasture fence with a wire stretcher, when the barbed wire snapped and recoiled on him, catching his arm between the end of his leather glove and rolled up shirt sleeve, tearing the gash across it. As the doctor applied a stinging red liquid to guard against infection and then bandaged the arm, Justyn tried to carry on a conversation with him.

"You certainly have a spacious building here. I'm surprised that with the main street location, other businesses haven't tried to lease space from you." Justyn was carefully fishing for confirmation of what he already suspected.

"I would love to rent part of my space, if someone was interested. So far no one has approached me on the idea. Are you aware of anyone who might be interested in renting some space here?"

"Not at the moment, but I'll sure keep my ears open for you." Justyn tried to sound nonchalant, but inside he was beginning to seethe.

"Now you take it easy on that arm for awhile. Barring infection, it should be good as new in a week."

"Thanks Doc. How much do I owe you?"

After settling the bill and stepping outside, Justyn allowed his mind to again zero in on the information just gleaned. So Jack hadn't made arrangements to set up a Reality office in town, as he had implied to Sara. Just what exactly was that slick panhandler up to now? Whatever it was, Justyn didn't like the feel of it. He sensed that 'when the shoe fell,' somehow Sara would be the victim.

As if to reinforce his premonition, Sara's pickup tore by at the very moment, roaring right through the four way stop on the corner by the clinic. The quick glimpse he had suggested that both truck and driver were not totally in control. Running to his own pickup, he jumped in and hit the starter. Nothing happened. He cranked the key again and heard nothing but a metallic sounding click. Slamming the steering wheel with his good hand and calling the vehicle all kinds of choice names, he clambered back out and yanked open the hood. He had meant to clean the battery posts some time ago, when the connection began giving hints of something less than full power. Now the procrastination had cost him dearly.

Rummaging through his toolbox that he pulled from behind the truck seat, Justyn found the half inch box end wrench and a wire brush. In ten minutes he had the cable connectors and battery posts corrosion free and reconnected to each other. In that ten minutes that seemed an eternity, Justyn had also had time to think. Sara had not exactly invited further interaction with him at their last meeting. In fact, she had downright discouraged their even being seen together. So should he going running after her now, even if she was distraught about something new? If his reputation became sullied with hers, would it adversely affect his horse sales, his livelihood? And even if he did go to see her, would she even talk to him, or simply send him packing with a slammed door in the face for his troubles?

Collecting his tools and slamming the hood a little harder than necessary, Justyn threw his toolbox back behind the seat, slammed the back of the seat back into position, climbed in and again cranked the key. This time the engine roared to life and he wrenched the stick shift into reverse. Still uncertain what to do as he backed out onto the street, Justyn chose to turn the corner and head for the Post Office to pick up his mail. He then came back to Main street and stopped at the grocery store for a few things he needed, before finally following the now cold trail of Sara's pickup. He would decide when he reached her lane whether to turn in or head straight on to his place.

Rounding a corner of the brush lined gravel road, Justyn noticed skid marks and then had to quickly hit his own brakes to narrowly miss a pickup precariously perched on the edge of the narrow gravel road. Coming to a grinding stop in a cloud of dust, Justyn spied Sara running back toward her vehicle, and now running towards his, a look of terror on her already tear-stained face. He barely had time to step out of his truck before she barreled into his arms and clung to him with all her might, sobbing almost hysterically.

Rubbing her back with his good arm, he continued to hold her and tried to soothe her. The closeness also stirred something deep within his own heart, melting away the guarded barriers he had so carefully placed there. In that moment he knew he would do anything to protect her, no matter what other people might think.

Gradually the sobbing slowed and Sara was able to regain some composure. Using the handkerchief Justyn offered her, she finally managed to articulate what had happened.

"I was probably driving a little faster than I should have," she paused to wipe her nose, "and when I hit this curve, my truck skidded a bit and then there was this loud bang. I guess the force was too much on my old tires and one of them blew. Coupling that with my momentum, the truck almost flipped over into the ditch. When it finally stopped at that awful slant, I just had to get out before it tipped over, even though I knew it was parked at an awful angle should anyone else come along. I just couldn't force myself to get back in to move it, so I started walking home" the latter was said through another jerking sob.

Realizing that where they were standing even now was still precarious, should another vehicle round the corner even at regular speed, Justyn took charge. A quick glance in the back of Sara's truck revealed no spare tire or jack, so he urged Sara into his own pickup and then quickly removed his own spare tire and jack, dropping both of them near her pickup.

"Now Sara, I know this may be very hard for you, but I need your help here. Let's put on the emergency flashes on this truck, and then I need you to back up until you can see around the corner back there. Stop there where they can see you to slow down any other traffic while I change your tire. I don't hear anyone else coming right now, so you will be safe in backing up. Stay there until I signal you. Can you do that for me? It just might save my life."

Nodding through a few last tears, Sara touched his face through the window to show her gratitude, sending a tingling sensation of pure delight up and down her spine, not to mention his. Combining that sensation with the powerful sense of finally being protected again by someone who genuinely cared, something the hug earlier had given her, it was all Sara could do to back the truck up straight and stay on the road until she was far enough around the corner to be seen from the other side.

Having watched her until safely stopped, Justyn now stooped to loosen the lug nuts on the blown tire. From her vantage point several hundred yards away, it appeared to Sara that he was favoring one arm as he worked. Even so, he still appeared extremely muscular and efficient as he jacked up the truck, removed the bad tire and replaced it with his own spare. In record time the job was done. He tossed her ruined tire, along with his jack and wheel wrench into her truck box on the upper side to help balance the vehicle, then gingerly climbed into the slanting cab and started the engine. Gently he maneuvered the vehicle back onto the center of the road, signally for her to come by waving his arm and then drove the half-mile to her lane. Pulling in, he drove the pickup to the spot in the yard where Sara usually parked it and stopped. As Sara pulled up alongside, Justyn had already retrieved his jack and wheel wrench, which he tossed into his own pickup box again.

It was an awkward moment as Sara climbed out of Justyn's truck and came to stand by him. Both individually knew something had changed within them but they did not know that something had also happened within the other. Neither wanted to be the first to risk revealing their newborn, still fragile feelings.

At last both started to say something at the same time and both stopped to wait for the other. Finally, at

Sara's encouraging smile, Justyn spoke, staying in a safe
area.

"I'm afraid that tire of yours is ruined. I could
probably salvage the rim for you, if I take the tire to my
house and separate the two. Then the shop in town could
mount another tire on it for you. They have some used
ones that should fit the bill" he finished rather lamely.

Nodding in assent to his plan, Sara now reiterated
what she had started to say.

"Could I at least make you a cup of coffee, as
payment for helping a damsel in distress?" It was good to
see her begin to smile again.

"Sounds good. I am a little thirsty after changing
that tire." Grabbing the ruined tire and tossing it into the
back of his pickup, he began subconsciously to rub his
injured arm, which Sara only now noticed to be bandaged
under his rolled down sleeve.

"What happened to your arm?" she asked, concern
edging her voice.

"Oh, just a little wire cut" and he went on to
explain what had happened as they walked to the house
and entered the kitchen, careful to keep a safe distance
between them.

Stoking up the coals still glowing red in the wood
stove, Sara added wood from the wood box, nursing them
back into a steady flame. When the chopped wood began
to crackle acceptably, she set about dumping out the old
coffee grounds, rinsing the pot, refilling it with fresh
water and coffee grounds and setting it on the hottest part
of the stove to perk. While they continued to chat about
neutral things, Justyn noticed how quickly and efficiently
she worked, without a wasted motion. He also could not
help but notice how pretty Sara was, despite being

somewhat disheveled right now, and how she brought a vibrancy to even this old, roughly built kitchen, something his kitchen, though more modern, clearly lacked.

But despite the buoyant appearance, as she placed a plate of homemade oatmeal cookies on the table and sat down across from him to wait for the coffee to perk, Justyn could also clearly see the stress and fatigue in her eyes and in the slump of her shoulders. Something more than the near accident was deeply troubling her and his newly surfaced, heartfelt compassion drove him to risk taking their conversation to a deeper level.

"Sara, when you ran into my arms out their on the road, it stirred powerful feelings within me that are two precious to ignore or keep to myself. More than anything, I wanted to protect you then, and I still do now. But I need to know what to protect you from, beyond the near accident from the blowout. Can you risk sharing with me what is going on?"

At that precise moment the coffee began to perk furiously, causing Sara to bounce to her feet and run to move it to a slightly cooler spot on the stove. The interruption also gave her time to organize her thoughts in a way that would minimize her risks. But as she returned to the table a few moments later with two mugs full of steaming coffee and again sat across from him, those big steal gray eyes conveyed such compassion, trust and yes, perhaps love, along with expectancy that all her reserve and guardedness simply melted away.

Two coffee refills and a well used handkerchief later, the whole story of Jack's trap was exposed, complete with details filled in from the things Justyn had learned.

"So Jack never ever planned to open an office in the first place. It was all just a ruse to get me into his home and ultimately take advantage of me. How could I have been so blind?" Sara lamented.

"Well, you needed a job and he seemed a legitimate option, the only opportunity around, in fact. You can't blame yourself for trying to earn money to pay your bills" Justyn tied to encourage her.

"I should have listened to Corrie, or you for that matter. You both saw right through Jack from the start, but I was too proud, wanting to make my own way so bad I let it cloud my own better judgment. Now my reputation is ruined and I still have no money to pay my bills." She began to sob again quietly.

"You know Sara," his voice was gentle, almost apologetic for breaking into her mourning, "I'm not much at praying in front of others, but I think we both need a strength beyond our own right now. You to work through this crisis and me to keep from going into town and busting Jack's head."

His hand had very gently and tentatively come to rest open on hers, not clutching like Jack had, but simply resting there.

"Could I try to pray for you, for us, right now Sara?"

Her eyes brimming with fresh tears, her throat too choked up for words to emerge, she simply nodded her head and then keep it bowed, her eyes closed. How preciously different this rugged man before her was, from the polished "gentleman" in town.

Sometime during the simple prayer time that followed, Sara had turned her hand over to entwine her fingers with Justyn's much larger ones.

"And Father, give us wisdom and help to be 'wise as a serpent, yet harmless as a dove' as we try to work our way out of this painful, difficult situation. Amen." They both echoed the amen together.

Little did the two new prayer partners know that even as they concluded their prayer time, at least part of the answer to that prayer was, at that very moment, knocking at Justyn's kitchen door, one mile away.

Chapter 24
The Pastor Comes Calling

Pastor Alden stood rapping loudly on the front door of Justyn's house. Receiving no response, he finally called out with his booming voice, "Justyn are you in there?" Still hearing no answering call, he decided to check the barn and around the farmyard. Used to visiting farming parishioners, he usually eventually found them in the near vicinity of the yard, working on one project or another.

But this time he came up dry and so returned to his vehicle disappointed. He had intended to provide some pastoral care and, in the process, discover the reason behind Justyn's seriousness and intensity after the service last Sunday.

Just as he was about to start his vehicle he heard a pickup approaching on the country road. His decision to wait to see if it would slow and turn into the farm driveway was rewarded.

"Hi Pastor Alden!" Justyn called warmly as he stepped out of his truck. "Did you just get here?"

"Actually, I had a few moments to check out your operation while looking for you," Pastor Alden's strong, yet gentle voice responded as he stepped back out from his car, a twinkle in his eye. The two men shock hands vigorously and went to sit on the veranda chairs in order to catch the lingering warm Fall weather.

After a few moments of chit chat, Pastor Alden singled out the reason for his pastoral call. "Justyn, on Sunday I sensed something agitating you, way down deep. My intention is not to pry into matters that do not concern me, but I would like to offer my help and support if it is a matter you would like to talk through with someone who cares."

Justyn remained silent for a full moment, debating within himself how much he could tell the Pastor without breaking confidentiality with Sara. Since Sara and he had not discussed boundaries on this issue, Justyn was somewhat at a loss as to know how to proceed.

As the silence lengthened, Pastor Alden was the first to speak up, somewhat uncomfortably. "I fully respect your right to privacy Justyn. Perhaps at another time you would be more ready to share what is on your heart." He made as to get up from his seat.

Motioning him to remain seated, Justyn quickly reassured his pastor. "It's not at all that I don't want to discuss this delicate matter with you Pastor. In fact, I would actually really appreciate your wisdom and insight on the matter. It's just that it involves someone else and I'm not sure how much I should disclose without her permission."

At the mention of "her" Pastor Alden raised an eyebrow in question. "Is this "her" someone I know? Could I visit with her too about this "situation?"

"You know what? That is a great idea. Give me a minute to place a quick phone call and I'll see is she can come over right now. Then you could hear the whole story in one sitting."

Pastor Alden nodded and settled back into his deck chair, speculating in his mind over just who the 'she' might be while Justyn went into the house to make the call.

The glossy black party line telephones were a wonderful new addition to the community, but Justyn would need to be careful in what he said to Sara over the phone, since up to ten neighbors shared the same line and any, or all, could also listen in to their not so private conversation.

When he first picked up the receiver, he heard someone else already on the line so he hung up and waited for what seemed like an especially long minute. Probably having heard his click when trying to get on the first time, the line was now clear but whoever had been on it would probably pick up again after the ring, just to hear who had interrupted their conversation and what was so important that the phone was needed.

Dialing Sara's number, which he had looked up while waiting, since he had not memorized it yet, Justyn now waited for the familiar two longs and a short ring that was Sara's. By the time the sequence rang a second time, he had figured out a diplomatic message, coded enough to throw off any others listening and yet communicating clearly enough to Sara. So when Sara answered he was all ready.

"Yah, this is Justyn, your neighbor to the south. I have someone here who I think could help us with that thing we discussed earlier. Could you come over and maybe the three of us can sit down, hash it all over and come up with a plan?"

Hesitating at first because of the decidedly casual, almost disinterested tone Justyn was using, Sara was just about to call him on it when she heard the little click on the line, signaling that someone else had picked up to listen in. Immediately she caught on to what he was trying to do and played along.

"I suppose we should deal with it now, rather than waiting for Spring." She was matching Justyn's boring tone beautifully. "Are you sure your visitor is knowledgeable enough in what we need to help us?" For all the world, or at least the part that was listening, both parties really tried to make it sound like some type of chore that needed to be done because of their adjoining properties.

"Oh yes, you appreciate his wisdom too. Could you come over right now?"

Sara agreed and hung up, curious to see who the mystery person was and if she really did know him, or her. Checking herself in the mirror and hastily pinning some straying curls back in place, she hurried out the door and made the quick trip to her "neighbor to the south's" yard. Seeing Pastor Alden's car there, as she drove up in her truck, filled her with both relief and apprehension. Could the Pastor really help them with this huge dilemma? And could they trust him with its sensitive nature?

Then another awful thought struck Sara with great force, terrifying her. Was Pastor Alden part of the church "camp" that had already judged and condemned her? As the terror struck home, it took all of her self-control to keep from spinning her truck around and dashing back down the driveway before she encountered him. But then she remembered her dangerously poor tires and here recent mishap with being in too much of a hurry. And she also realized that it was too late anyway. Both men had already noticed her and rose to greet her. Would she trust her newly declared friend's judgment on this meeting? Would she trust the God the other man represented?

Swallowing a big lump of uncertainty in her throat, Sara coasted to a stop and shut off her engine. Before everything was entirely quiet, Justyn was already opening her door and offering to assist her out of the high truck.

All the while her eyes, having now made contact, never left Pastor Alden's. As she drew closer to him, she just had to know where he stood, and the first sign of his answer would be in his eyes so she continued to look directly into them. But all that was there spoke of warmth and acceptance. There wasn't even a hint of a judgmental attitude or of aloofness. His warm greeting and firm handshake, all of which helped to calm Sara's jittery nerves considerably, further reinforced the genuine caring.

The trio entered Justyn's house, to give a further sense of privacy, and they scooted the kitchen chairs into a semi-circle, more conducive to intimate conversation. After a few moments of discussing how Corrie was doing in school, Sara took the plunge and directed the conversation to the heart of the issue, something Justyn had sincerely hoped she would take the lead and do when she was ready.

"I suppose you have heard the character damaging rumors around town about me?" she dared to ask, now trusting her long time friendship with the Pastor to carry her through.

A look of compassion, coupled with pain, settled on Pastor Alden's face.

"Yes, I am afraid I have. Much of what is being said is very damaging to your integrity, not to mention to your Christian witness," the Pastor stated resignedly.

With a slight clearing of her throat, Sara moved to the edge of her seat to better hear the next response that would impact her entire future in this community.

"And do you believe there is any truth in the rumors you have heard?" At the plea for acceptance obvious in her troubled blue eyes, Pastor Alden took a deep breath and actually smiled.

"Sara, I have far more faith in you, and in our God working within you, then I do in crude rumors going around our town. I give you full credit for the honest way you have lived your life ever since I met you. As a result, I still believe in you and trust you. Now, that having been cleared up, why don't you tell me what actually happened, so we can work from the truth, rather than greatly embellished lies? I assume you are comfortable telling your story in front of your good neighbor here?" He smiled at both appreciatively as they too relaxed a bit more and nodded.

With the supportive encouragement of both caring men, Sara began again to tell her painful story. Although she broke down twice in the telling, the gentle support allowed her time to compose her self and continue. Justyn even jumped in occasionally to add a detail he had unearthed or to appropriately clarify a point for the Pastor. By the time the whole situation was exposed, right down to the deceitful marriage proposal, all three had tears in their eyes.

Hurriedly brushing his away, Justyn now spoke up more strongly, anger now tingeing his voice. "Couldn't we as a church discipline Jack in some way for this despicable thing he has done? If we put enough pressure on him, we might be able to kick him out of the community and ruin his business enough so he can never sell real estate here again!" Justyn was now on his feet shouting, his desire for revenge pulsating throughout his entire body.

"Calm down, calm down" Pastor Alden admonished, having also stood to rest his hand on Justyn's muscular shoulder in order to gently push have back down on to his seat. "The last thing we need is more abusive behavior. Now let's talk this through with calmer heads."

After the two men had settled back down into their chairs, Pastor Alden began to lay out the situation from his broader perspective.

"Firstly Justyn, you know that if we go into this thing purely run by anger and the desire for revenge, we lower ourselves to the same despicable level that Jack has used. We can't afford to do that, for it would greatly dishonor our God."

"Secondly, although Jack indeed does darken our doors on occasion at church, he has never chosen to become a member. As a result, the church cannot formally discipline him."

Sensing Justyn was about to interrupt, Pastor Alden waved him off by raising his hand, palm forward, and then continued. "Thirdly, we must work to restore Sara's reputation, not just tear down Jack's, leaving them both shredded."

Sighing and finally nodding in agreement, Justyn again settled back in his seat. "You are right, of course. What you say makes sense. But what can we do to make things right again?"

"The task is very daunting, to be sure. Things may never be totally right again, in the same way they were before. Counteracting rumors is like trying to re-stuff a broken feather pillow in the middle of a windstorm. Some feathers will be lost, as will the trust of some people in this situation. Trust is a fragile thing, but for the most part, it can be earned and restored. We need to pray earnestly, beseeching our great God for a plan that can do the most good in the shortest time. Will you join me in such a prayer, right now?"

Two heads immediately nodded simultaneously and the trio knelt together while the local shepherd appealed to the Great Shepherd for wisdom and grace for such a time as this. When the prayer time was complete, tears again glistened in three sets of eyes, but behind those tears was a distinct sense of peace, for the God of justice and peace had made it clear that he too, was on their side.

Chapter 25
The Change

Pastor Alden's strategy for destroying the rumor mill about Sara was simple enough. On the following Sunday he preached a powerful sermon about the sin of gossip. "Especially when it is used to murder a fellow believer's reputation," he thundered from the pulpit, "it is the very tool of Satan himself."

At the gasps of astonishment throughout the congregation, he gentled his voiced and tone. "Now if you think I am being a little too strong on this issue, see for yourself what the Holy Scriptures have to say. Paul states the matter just as dramatically in Romans chapter one. Listen to him describe gossip and its just end. Let us begin in vs. 29 of Romans 1:

Being filled with all unrighteousness, fornication, wickedness, covetousness, maliciousness--that's one form of gossip, isn't it? The list goes on—full of envy, murder, debate, deceit, malignity; whisperers—there it is again, gossip—Backbiters, haters of God, despiteful, proud, boasters, inventors of evil things—that could be gossip too, couldn't it?—disobedient to parents—that's quite a list of awful sins, isn't it? And what does Paul declare as the deserving end of such sin? Go down to vs. 32: Who knowing the judgment of God, that they which commit such things are worthy of death, not only do the same, but have pleasure in them and do them" (Romans 1:29,30,32).

What is Paul saying here? He says that those that practice these sins are worthy of death. Now that is a pretty serious punishment, don't you think? Does he mean that only the one who practices all of these sins combined deserved to die? No, Paul states that whenever we do anything that we know goes against God's ways, we deserve to die for it. Now did you notice that gossip is right in the middle of these other awful sins? You see, God does not see sins in levels of graduated wickedness. Rather he sees sin as sin, and God views gossip as squarely on this list of unacceptable behaviors, deserving death.

That means that in God's eyes those who gossip among us deserve death!"

This time no one dared glance about during the message and especially not in Sara's direction for they had a foreboding of what was about to come.

"Now it has been brought to my attention that malicious gossip has been spreading in this very church," Pastor Alden declared firmly, causing further stirring and murmurs among the people, "First, I intend to eradicate the outright lies by exposing them with the truth, just as Scripture calls me to do, and then I will call you to repentance, all who have passed on the lie, or believed it, without bothering to check the rumor for truth. What I am about to share comes by permission of our dear, wounded fellow believer.

To introduce the story, allow me to use the same illustration Nathan used to confront King David about his sin with Bathsheba. Nathan described how a poor farmer had only one lamb to his name, which he raised in the house with his children, as a highly loved family pet. One day his wealthy neighbor, who owned two hundred sheep, had a guest arrive unexpectedly. Not willing to butcher an animal from his own herd, he snatched the poor man's only lamb, the family pet, slaughtered it and prepared it for his guest's meal.

'Who is this man?' King David demanded! 'He deserves a great punishment!' 'You are the man,' Nathan replied, and went on to explain how David had stolen Uriah's only wife Bathsheba." Pastor Alden paused for a pregnant moment, to let the story sink in. Then with calm but authoritative words, he brought the story home.

"You are the ones. You are the people who have recklessly slaughtered the reputation of one of our own faithful sisters." Then in the same serious tone he went on to explain the working arrangement Sara and Jack had set up, thereby explaining the innocence of their being seen together frequently at his home. Then he proceeded to describe, in discrete detail, the false rumors that had been spread about, concerning the supposed nature of this relationship, making a special point to include those youth who had 'shared' at High School.

When he finished, there was scarcely a dry eye in the place. Many heads hung in shame.

"Now we cannot simply take back the rumors we have helped spread, for gossip cannot be reclaimed. The damage has already been done. But here is what we can do. First, let us confess to God our sinful and shameful involvement in this gossip and, second, let us seek forgiveness and reconciliation with the one we have wronged. I invite you to come forward now, to publicly declare your confession to God and then to reconcile with Sara and her daughter Corrie, as they stand with me, to meet you here at the foot of Christ's cross."

The church had not previously seen traffic up the aisle like happened that morning. While a few stoic faces remained in there seats or left, most followed Mrs. Talkaday who was the very first one up the aisle. With tear stained faces reconciliation was made, first with God, then with Sara and Corrie, and warm hugs were shared all around. It is said that confession is good for the soul. Well, that Sunday the entire church was blessed with a unity and oneness that can only come by purging sin from the camp.

Restitution was made all the more sweet two days later, when a check arrived in the mail for Sara. It was from Jack and covered not only the $100 he had promised her, but also an additional $50 bonus. Mrs. Talkaday later confided with Pastor Alden to being approached by Jack, who pretended to share, in utmost confidence of course, that Sara might be pregnant. Before he could even spit out that he had intended to do right by her, Mrs. Talkaday had lit into him with such a tongue lashing, that even Jack was cowed. And if that wasn't enough, though Pastor Alden had been careful to avoid incriminating Jack in the message, several local businessmen in the congregation had pieced together that part of the story and applied pressure on Jack to pay his debts. They also made it very clear to him that, as a local businessman, he was clearly on probation in the small community, until he again proved himself a person of integrity.

Unable to stand such scrutiny however, or change his unscrupulous ways, within two weeks Jack had packed up and moved lock, stock and barrel, to Grande Prairie, in the hopes that the larger center would give him anonymity and be more accepting of his preferred style. The very next day, as if in response to his departure, or to more permanently keep him from returning, the first winter storm of the year hit with a vengeance, dumping an entire foot of snow together with freezing temperatures all over the Peace Country. Yes, winter had indeed arrived in all its fury, threatening to destroy any weakness it could find in its wake.

Chapter 26
The Past Comes Calling

As she watched the driving force of the sandy ice crystals blast against her living room window, Sara could not help but let a great sigh escape from her tight lips. Yes, her livestock was safe in the new cattle shed, things were definitely better at church and even for Carrie at school, but Sara's essential problem still remained. She was facing a severe winter with no means of income. Even the farmland lay at rest, with no prospect of producing any kind of cash for at least eight months. Then there would be the need for money for seed and for planting. How would Corrie and her ever survive?

"Fear not, for I am with you!"

Where had that thought come from? It sounded like a Bible verse. Was it really a promise from God, for her personally? As the precious thought settled in, it helped to keep the black net of despair from settling over her and totally ensnaring her. Focusing her thoughts upon her caring community pushed more blackness back. Justyn's image, in particular, flashed to her mind and Sara couldn't help but smile, a warm feeling suddenly spreading throughout her entire body. Since the tire episode, and the prayer trio with Pastor Alden, Sara and Justyn had a new understanding. Though no formal commitment yet existed, they were seeing each other on a regular, planned basis now. One such regular event was Sunday dinner, which they took turns hosting, and to which they included only Corrie. It was their "family" time as they sought to build a three-way network. Then, just for the two of them, there were drop in visits, another horseback ride or two, and even a movie night complete with supper out, in the neighboring town of High Prairie, some 60 miles north and east of Valleyview.

And so, while both adults wanted to proceed slowly and carefully, both were becoming more and more comfortable with the idea of fully sharing life together. Without a doubt, their commitment to each other was silently growing.

"Yes, it is only a matter of time," Sara mused to herself, "but can I keep ends together until the time is right?" She continued to watch out the window for the school bus hopeful it would arrive before the storm worsened.

***

Even on the bus ride home, Corrie was already restless and the prospect of being snowed in didn't help matters one little bit. "Sure, this early storm maybe would result in missing a day or two of school if the school buses couldn't run," she mused to herself, "but she still would be stuck inside their little farm house for the duration, with nothing more exciting to do than try to keep warm. Staying warm. Now that was a challenge in itself, especially when the wind blew from the north as it was currently. Somehow it just seemed to come right on through the poorly insulated farmhouse walls. In fact, when it was really cold, ice crystals formed on the inside of the walls and they just radiated coldness toward anyone or anything within a foot of them."

It was at times like this that Corrie envied her friends in town, snug in their warm, new houses. Even some of the other farmhouses, like Uncle Justyn's, were better built, not to mention roomier.

"If only Justyn would pop the question, I'm sure Mom would say yes. Then we could move out of our drafty old place and into his nice ranch house," Corrie mumbled to herself as they neared her corner, drawing a questioning look from the person riding beside her, who heard the mumble but, fortunately, not the content.

"Never mind" Corrie sighed and then quickly added, "Just talking to myself."

Gathering her books and lunch kit, she lurched to her feet as the bus slid to a stop at the end of her driveway. "See you tomorrow!" she called back to her friends, as she trudged down the aisle, out the open door and into the blistery storm. "The way this storm is building, if I'm not here within fifteen minutes of my regular time tomorrow, I won't be coming" the bus driver told her as she exited.

Pulling up the hood on her coat to at least somewhat protect her from the wind and blowing snow, Corrie was grateful for the lingering daylight that at least made the farmhouse visible amidst the swirling snow. Bracing herself to walk against the north wind, she plowed through the three inches of snow already accumulated, as she made her way to the farmhouse steps. She would need to change clothes, bundle up more warmly and then check on the livestock before darkness fell and the storm intensified. If the conditions worsened, even that simple job would become dangerous, if not impossible.

***

Justyn was also braving the biting wind and blowing snow, to make sure his horses were safely sheltered from the elements. The mares carrying spring foals he had placed inside his horse barn as well as the younger stock.

The colts and fillies, almost yearlings now, had filled out nicely and were lively bundles of nervous energy as they sensed the imminent worsening of the storm. It took some effort to coax them into the inner paddock. Securely latching their gate, Justyn double-checked the horses left outside but kept in the closest corrals so the barn frame would give them some shelter from the driving storm and the sturdy corral rails would keep them from drifting away with the lashing wind, should a whiteout occur.

Finally satisfied that all was secure in the farmyard, Justyn fought his way back to the house, periodically beating his arms against his sides and rubbing his hands together to retain circulation. Somehow the first storm of the year was always the hardest to handle. Over the summer a person's body forgot how to cope with intense cold and so those first icy blasts seemed to penetrate to the very bone. First task once inside, would be to crank up the oil heater and then go in search of his winter duds, including his long johns.

As he fought to keep his screen door from being ripped out of his hand and off its hinges by the severe wind, he couldn't help but wander if his neighbors to the west were prepared for this vicious onslaught of winter. He knew their house was not that well built and with the wood stove being their only source of heat, it would take constant attention, day and night, if it were to effectively fight off the creeping frost. Then too, he should have rigged up a rope from the house to the cattle shed, so they had something to follow if they had to check on the animals if the storm didn't let up for several days. Chiding himself for missing this important task, he made a mental note to take care of that little job at the earliest possibility.

Finally stepping inside and latching his door securely, Justyn stomped the clinging snow from his boots and tried to brush off what he could from his coat. Hanging it up, he headed directly for the oil stove in order to thaw him self out, bending down to crank it up a notch in an effort to hurry the process.

"Sure would be nice to have someone here to welcome me, have the house warm and filled with the savory aroma of supper cooking," he mused, his deep longing causing him to say it out loud to the empty house over the sound of the wind as it whistled around the eaves.

Immediately his thoughts were again back on Sara and his deep desire to share their lives together almost overwhelmed him. Here was a woman who shared his great love for the Peace country, who felt at home around farm animals and with country living, and who, best of all, loved his God as deeply as he himself had grown to love him. It just had to be God's will for them to become one in marriage. So what was holding him back from making the proposal? Was it fear of rejection, of spoiling something that had become so beautiful and precious? Was it fear that Sara, or he, was not yet ready to trust another human being so fully as committed marriage and their personal values required?

The jangling of the telephone savagely interrupted Justyn's moment of deep soul searching. Two shorts and one long. That was his ring. Who would be calling him in the middle of a storm? Fear coursed through him as his mind flashed to the vulnerable women next door. Had something already happened to them in the storm?

With his heart in his throat, he grabbed the receiver, his knuckles white, as he just barely managed to croak out "Hello?"

Rather than a familiar voice, or a hysteric one, the person on the other end sounded young, yet was a voice Justyn had never heard before.

"Is this Justyn Smyth?" the stranger calmly asked.

"Yes, I'm Justyn" he managed to stammer, relieved that it wasn't Sara or Corrie, yet still greatly mystified as to who this could be.

"Are you the same Justyn Smyth that used to live in Edmonton, and then worked in the oil patch for awhile?" the voice questioned further.

Growing somewhat wary now, Justyn responded somewhat hesitantly, "Yes, I have been in those places." And then mustering up his courage, he jumped in with his own question. "Who is calling please?" he asked, trying to move from the defensive to the offensive.

"My name is Amanda. You don't know me but I was wondering if you knew my mother? Her name is Jane Anne. She told me a lot about her special friend, Justyn Smyth. If you are the same person, I would really like to meet you," the voice concluded sweetly.

Totally blown away by this unexpected intrusion from his almost forgotten past, Justyn simply went silent for a moment, trying to collect his rattled thoughts and figure out how to respond.

"Hello, are you still there?" the gentle voice interrupted his reminiscing.

"Yes, I'm still here, and yes, I did know a Jane Anne Wilson some fifteen years ago, but I have never heard from her since. You say she is your mother?" Justyn couldn't quite keep the incredulity from his voice. Now

his mind was beginning to click as he began to remember
Jane Anne's exodus from his own life and the later rumor
that she had become pregnant. Could this really be her
daughter? And why in the world was she contacting him?

"Yes, Jane Anne Wilson is, or was, my mother." The
voice became even softer. "She died this summer with
pyrosis of the liver. One of her dying requests was that I
try and find you as someone she remembered as a true
friend. It took me several months to pursue leads that I
found from her other old friends. Finally one of them
mentioned they had heard you had eventually moved up
to the Valleyview area. So I came up here on the bus and
found your name in the phone book. Would you be
willing to come and at least meet me?" The last part came
out in a rush of hope and expectancy, as if she was
holding her breath in waiting for his response.

Her lengthy monolog had give Justyn enough time to
at least somewhat compose himself. Truth be told, right
now he didn't know what to feel or think. At first it had
sounded like an old flame was about to reenter his life.
Now, upon hearing she was dead, a sharp sadness had
settled on his heart, replacing the old feeling of
excitement and surprising even him. Jane Anne and he
had been very close. He at least owed it to that memory,
to meet the person claiming to be her daughter.

"I would like to meet you Amanda," Justyn quietly
responded, trying to add warmth to his voice, "but I am
afraid we will need to wait until this storm blows over. Do
you have a safe place to stay in the mean time?" The
caring he felt for this complete stranger seemed a little
unsettling to him.

"I checked in to the Sandman Inn, on the west end of
town but it's kind of expensive for me. Do you think the

storm will last long?" Amanda inquired, worry tingeing her voice.

"It might blow itself out overnight," Justyn replied in a comforting tone, though unsure what he said would actually hold true. "In any case, I will come in as soon as the storm is over and the roads are plowed out. Town will be plowed before our country roads but I live on a school bus route, so my road should be cleared shortly after theirs. I'll call just before I head in. I assume if I call the Inn and give your name, they would forward the call to your room?"

Justyn even heard Amanda let out her breath and now delight edged her voice. "That would be wonderful! Thank you so much for being willing to meet me Mr. Smyth. My mother was right about you. I really appreciate this and I look forward very much to meeting you after the storm."

Not quite sure what else to say, Justyn mumbled something in response, said goodbye and hung up the phone. Still in somewhat of a daze, he began to second-guess himself. Should he have agreed to meet her? Was this for real or was it some kind of set up? Should he take someone with him when he went, just in case? She did have the names and dates right? Should he have asked for more information, even a description of Jane Anne, just to be sure?

As it turned out, the storm lasted well into the next day and it wasn't until the following morning that the roads were finally plowed out. That gave Justyn two nights and a whole day, stranded inside by the storm, to stew over this new turn of events in his life. His thoughts had taken him through the entire gambit from "this is all a mistake and I am not the Justyn Smyth she is looking for" to "what if she needs financial support. She must be only about 15. Do I owe her anything just because I knew her Mom?" The battle had raged on in his mind, abating only for the few moments during which he struggled out to the barn to feed the horses and return. Even a phone call to check on Sara and Corrie, who were managing fine and promising to stay inside until the storm abated, failed to deter his thinking for long. He had been on the verge of telling Sara abut his dilemma, to at least have someone to talk it through with, but at the last second had decided against it. He told himself it was because of the phone party line and the potential of someone else listening in and starting a rumor mill. On the surface at least, this sounded like a legitimate concern, but underneath a small part of Justyn was not yet ready to share with anyone painful moments from his past, especially if it might jeopardize his currently developing, still fragile, romance. That split second decision of remaining mute was one he would come to greatly regret.

Chapter 27
Borrowed for a Time

The insistent ringing of his telephone interrupted Pastor Alden's breakfast. Now that the roads were plowed out, he had hoped to check on some of his congregation, in case they needed additional help digging out. He was one who was never afraid to make his pastoral care very practical, especially for the elderly who should not be shoveling snow. "Who might be needing me now?" he mused to himself, as he went to pick up the receiver. He was pleasantly surprised to hear Justyn's voice on the other end of the line.

After a few moments of chit chat regarding the storm, Justyn got right to the point. "Pastor, I wonder if I might borrow you for about half an hour this morning?"

Intrigued by the request, as well as how it was stated, Pastor Alden chuckled and said, "I am happy to be of help in whatever way I can, Justyn. Just what exactly do you mean, borrow me?"

"I need to go meet someone in town and I would like you to go along. Can you be ready in twenty minutes? I'll fill you in on the details when I get there."

"I've learned to trust you on these little adventures, Justyn. One thing I'll say. Life is never boring with you around. I'll be ready when you get here."

Hanging up the phone, Pastor Alden explained to his wife about the mystery mission, quickly finished his breakfast and was shaved, dressed and ready to go when Justyn pulled into the parsonage driveway.

Climbing into the warm cab of Justyn's pickup, the Pastor teasingly confronted the man he affectionately considered like a son.

convinced him Jane Anne would be older now, that she was in fact deceased, and that this must be Amanda.

Timidly looking up and noticing his searching eyes rest on her with a start, Amanda slowly stood to her feet, casually maneuvered to keep a large chair between her and the two men, and then cautiously called out, "Are one of you Justyn Smyth?"

Equally wary, Justyn simply nodded and said, "You must be Amanda. I can't believe how much you look like your Mom, at least back when I knew her." He felt a hint of a blush working up his neck and cheeks.

"Then you are the right Justyn Smyth. I am thrilled to meet you! Thanks for coming!" Coming out from behind the chair all smiles, she still shook his hand somewhat gingerly, glancing at the gentleman beside him.

Remembering his manners, Justyn quickly introduced Pastor Alden and asked if she would like to accompany them to a restaurant for breakfast. When her face still registered some concern about going off with two men whom she had only just met, Justyn was heartened by her carefulness, especially given her young age, and assured her they could walk the one block, in plain sight, to the restaurant.

Taking a moment to run to her room to collect her coat and purse, Amanda rejoined the men in the lobby and lead the way out the door, as Justyn held it open for her. Then Pastor Alden took the lead, while Justyn and Amanda silently walked side-by-side, careful not to touch each other, as they followed him. Perhaps it was the cold that kept them from having much to say in the five-minute walk to their destination; perhaps it was the uncertainty of newness. In either case, silence reigned until the restaurant was reached and the three were ushered to a booth.

Since Pastor Alden had already eaten, he only ordered coffee. This freed him to socialize with Amanda and Justyn while they ate, something he was better at than Justyn. Over the next fifteen minutes he was able to help them become better acquainted by making it safe for each of them to tell their story.

Finally, during a momentary lull in the conversation during which their coffee mugs were being refilled, Amanda mustered up the courage to speak directly to Justyn. "I suppose you have been wondering why I tried so hard to find you?"

"I must admit that thought has crossed my mind a time or two since you first called me" Justyn responded, making the understatement of the year, for it had plagued him every waking moment. "Why is meeting me so important to you?"

Amanda looked down for a moment, as if gathering her courage and then looked Justyn directly in the eye with an unwavering intensity. "I wanted to meet you because I think you might be my father!" she finally blurted out.

The waitress, a high school friend of Corry's, almost dropped the cream pitcher she had just refilled, as she overheard this last comment. Embarrassed, she quickly placed it on the table and left. Too stunned to even notice her, both Justyn and Pastor Alden sat with their mouths open, starring at Amanda. Pastor Alden was the quickest to recover.

"Oh my, that is quite a bombshell to drop on us Amanda. What lead you to believe that Justyn possibly is your dad?"

"Well, Mom always talked about him in a very positive light. She dated a lot of losers while I was growing up and it got a lot worse when she started drinking. But whenever she mentioned the name Justyn Smyth, a warm light came into her eye for that moment that she reminisced, and then she would talk about how she should never have left the love of her life."

"As I grew up, this same scenario replayed itself countless times. Then, on her death bed, she made me promise to try and find you, Justyn. 'He is a good man, Amanda' she said. 'He will do right by you.' That is what made me think that maybe you are my dad." Amanda sighed deeply. "I guess I really wanted to believe that I really did belong to someone who actually cared about me. I even prayed about it for weeks. Am I wrong to at least ask?" The last was asked with tears gleaming in her eyes, as she looked pleadingly at first one man, than the other.

Chapter 28
Small Town Grapevine

The phone rang and Corrie answered it. "Corrie, I'm so glad you answered the phone," gushed the voice of one of her friends from school. "You will never guess what I just overheard!"

Still a little groggy from having slept in, Corrie mumbled, "Donna, what in the world are you going on about. Calm down a bit and tell me the story."

"Well, okay. I'll try." Taking a deep breath, Donna continued, "I am working the morning shift at the restaurant. I'm calling you on my break. Anyway, guess who showed up here for breakfast?"

"I have no clue," Corrie mumbled, becoming slightly disgusted with Donna's bubblyness and pending gossip.

"It was Justyn Smyth and he had a young girl with him, about your age!"

This information did penetrate Corrie's fogginess and sparked some interest.

"Okay, so who was she?"

"I have no idea!" Donna retorted. "That's what so freaky. I've never seen her before. She's not from around here."

"So what was she doing with Justyn?" Corrie was feeling just a little defensive now.

"That's what I have been trying to tell you Corrie!" Donna sounded exasperated now. She could hardly stand it that Corrie kept interrupting her big news.

"I was just returning to their table with fresh cream for their coffee when I heard this girl say that Justyn was her father!" This latter outburst was met with stunned silence. "Corrie, are you still there? Corrie, say something! What do you think about all this?"

Corrie was just too shocked for words. Finally she was able to stammer out, "Are you sure you heard right Donna?"

"Of course I'm sure!" came the prompt response. "That's exactly what I heard. Isn't that just too much? I mean, Mr. eligible bachelor himself. Do you suppose Justyn has a wife somewhere too, that we just don't know about yet? Well, I need to get back to work. See you at school." She hung up abruptly, before Corrie could comment further.

Which probably was a good thing, for a dark cloud of anger and depression began to settle over Corrie. "How could Justyn do this to my mom, and to me?" she began to fume. He had seemed so honest and sincere and all this while . . .

Her dark thoughts were interrupted by her Mom's voice from the other room. "Who was that, honey?" The question seemed to drift lazily from her mother's bedroom.

"Oh, it was for me. It just was Donna with some news; nothing earth shaking," Corrie responded, purposely vague. She was still trying to get her mind around what she had just heard.

"What kind of news?" the voice persisted, as its bearer now entered the room and looked directly at her daughter. For a moment Corrie panicked. It was one of those upside down moments when a child feels the need to protect their parent. Should she keep the news to herself, especially if it might not be true, or should she share with her mother information that would no doubt be devastating to them and to their future?

But before Corrie could make up her mind theoretically, the tears simply began to flow. There was just no way she could stop them. Faster and faster they came as the grief intensified. All the hopes and dreams she had of having a real dad and a secure home had just blown up in her face. How could this loss be happening again? How could they both be loosing their best friend and their bright future, all at the same time, just like the day her birth dad had died?

Sara held her daughter until the sobbing began to subside, a strange sense of foreboding settling in the pit of her stomach. What news could have so greatly upset Corrie? Had someone been injured or killed in the storm? Was there an accident of some kind among her friends?

Suddenly another harsh thought burst to the foreground of her mind. Was Justyn okay? The potency of that last thought rather startled even her and her heart jumped into her throat. But why would Donna call, if it was something about Justyn, her mind tried to reason.

Shaking herself from this grime revere, Sara forced calm into her voice as she began to gently question her daughter.

"Can you tell me about this news from Donna that has you so upset?" she gently questioned.

For a few moments Corrie pretended she was too upset to speak, but soon she just could not pretend any longer. Anger finally edged out her grief and all that Donna had said about Justyn and "his daughter" poured out. Nothing could have prepared Sara for this news. She was so shocked her whole being went numb as she slumped to a nearby chair, her head in her hands.

"This was the end then" Sara brooded over a cup of tea some time later that morning. "The end of a promising relationship, the end of their bright hope for the future, the end of trying to save the farm, the end of any real reason to stay in Valleyview. All gone because of one little conversation, overheard by a zealous teenager, in a noisy restaurant. Somehow this devastating news did something that the costly fire, the defamation of her character earlier that year, even fighting all the insurmountable odds had not done. It caused Sara to give up hope. And with the loss of hope, she plummeted into depression. The impending blackness was only further compounded by the long hours of winter darkness, common to the region, starting at four in the afternoon and lasting until nine the next morning. Not sure she could again handle sending Corrie out to the school bus in the dark and having her return home in the dark, Sara's depression influenced her to make a rash decision.

Purposely avoiding Justyn over the next few days, so as not to hear his rejection directly, she arranged to sell her remaining stock for travel money, put her land up for sale at the town office, and left the final details to be handled by the bank. Within two days mother and daughter had packed up what they wanted to keep, sold or gave away what they didn't need, and left what they couldn't get rid of to be sold with the farm, including the farm machinery and old pickup. Thus, by the end of the week, mother and daughter stood at the Greyhound bus depot with all their earthly possessions in four, overstuffed suitcases. Their plan was to go as far as Edmonton first, the Province's capital, some two hundred miles south, and if they could not find a way to make a living there, they would go another 180 miles further south to Calgary. Between these two large cities, they would find some kind of work. It really didn't matter where they ended up, they both had reasoned, as long as it got them away from Valleyview. And so the two were gone before most people in the community, and even the church, knew they were leaving.

Chapter 29
Women Hunt

After at least partially recovering from the shock of having met Amanda, who looked incredibly like his old flame Jane Anne, and her equally shocking news that he might be a father, Justyn spent the next couple of days trying to plan his life around this new potential responsibility.

First he made sure she had enough money to stay on at the Inn for the balance of the week. Then he did his best to have at least one meal together with her each day, so they could become better acquainted. Finally he had her out to his ranch, to show her around and introduce her to his world. Still uncertain how to combine his two worlds now, he chose to avoid saying anything about Sara or Corrie, nor did he arrange a meeting with them, though he knew he really wanted to tell them the whole story face to face, at some time in the future. If he tried a partial story now, they would read it in his eyes that there was some further connection with Amanda. He had to sort that part out for himself first, and decide what he was going to do. So he stayed away and in those few days of avoidance, his whole life changed right under his nose, without him even knowing it.

**

Slowly a new routine emerged and as the week with Amanda drew to an end, Justyn had determined two things. One, they would take a blood test to see if they actually were related. This idea Amanda had willingly agreed to do. Second, Justyn would go over to Sara's on

Saturday and put up that rope to the cattle shed, so they would be ready when the next winter blizzard hit.

Though the two-point plan was good, things immediately started to slide down hill. First, the doctor told them the blood samples would need to be sent to Edmonton for comparison and it would be at least two weeks before any results would be returned. That left Amanda and Justyn in a quandary as to what to do for the immediate present.

Then Justyn had the brain wave about asking Sara if Corrie and her could take Amanda in as a boarder for a couple of weeks. The cash would help them out, he would make sure Amanda was properly cared for, and it would all be a win/win situation. After all, he wouldn't even really need to tell them about his possible relationship to Amanda until the truth had been established.

And so it was with high spirits that Justyn drove into Sara and Corrie's yard that Saturday morning, only to be struck by an intense feeling of isolation. It was very quiet, too quiet, as he stepped out of his vehicle.

"Perhaps they are just in town, doing some grocery shopping" he spoke out loud to the empty yard, just to dispel the quietness. But the words didn't sound convincing, even to him. Instead, the sickening feeling in the pit of his stomach began to intensify. Then his keen eyes picked up further signs that something more serious was afoot. Subconsciously he had noticed, when driving in, that there were no new tire tracks in the fresh one-inch snowfall of last night. Now he noticed no footprints leading to the barn. Even the drift that had made its way onto the porch had not been swept away yet.

Stepping over the four-inch drift, he rapped loudly on the door, only to hear the hollow sound reverberate around him. He stomach lurched again as he knocked a second time, not really expecting a response this time. And, or course, there was no answer. He tried looking in a window but they were too frosted over on the inside to give him much chance to see anything.

"Why don't they have the heat turned up higher," he muttered to himself as he decided to try the door. It was firmly locked. Now the hair along the back of his neck began to prickle. What could have happened? Had one or the other gotten desperately sick? Did someone break in and hurt them?

His mind began to race with all the worst possibilities and Justyn had to forcibly calm himself. Again his eye saw no sign of forced entry so his mind tried to focus on the implications of that news. He began to whisper a prayer for their safety as he began to walk back out to his truck. As he swung his door open, he took a quick glance up at the chimney of the old farmhouse. There was no sign of smoke, which further confirmed no heat inside.

Nearly ready to panic now, the rancher's heightened senses picked up something else or, more specifically, something that was not there. He had noticed the eerie quietness when he first climbed out of his truck. Now he knew what was missing. There was no sound of livestock, not a neigh of a horse or a grunt of a pig. No cow announcing she needed to be milked. Instead, all was deathly quiet.

Hastily making his way to the new cattle shed, his worst fears were confirmed. There was not a living animal in sight. Then he noticed some older tracks that appeared as if a pickup had backed in and loaded up the livestock.

Squatting down in the sheltered part of the shed to study them more closely, he noticed that the right side truck tire had left a rather distinct tread mark. Perhaps he could follow it in order to find some answers. That the truck had made at least two trips should be of some help.

Jumping back into his pickup, he carefully drove out to the end of the driveway, watching for more signs of the unusual tire tread. He stopped about 50 yards back from the intersection and walked from there. He needed to see if he could spot which way the loaded pickup had turned. With the new skiff of snow it was harder, but Justyn's trained eye picked up the unique indentation on the shoulder of the driveway, where the road was still a little soft and the extra weight of the loaded truck made the track deeper. It turned away from the direction of his place and went in the opposite direction instead. Walking back to his truck, he also turned in that direction and drove slowly to the next intersection, watching for any other possible turnoff. Careful inspection of the next intersection revealed no trace of the vehicle having turned, so Justyn drove on to the next one-mile crossing. Here the track clearly turned right.

"That's funny," Justyn thought. "This road leads to the Brown's place. I haven't really visited with them since we built the cattle shed together for Sara. It's time I dropped in on them, just in case they can shed light on what has happened." Ironically, as he turned into the Brown's driveway, he noticed the same distinct tire tread had turned in here as well.

Pulling up to the house, he jumped out and hollered, "Hello, the Browns! Anyone home!" in a tone far more jovial then he felt. A responding shout came from both the house and the barn. Mrs. Brown poked her beaming face out of the door and called out, "Welcome Justyn. I'll put the coffee on. Lars is in the barn checking on our new stock. After you see them too, both of you come in for a snack."

Justyn nodded and turned toward the barn. Lars was already standing in the big double door entryway waiting for him.

"What is this about new stock?" Justyn questioned.

Lars just smiled and said, "Come see for yourself" as he led the way, having no idea that Justyn was still totally in the dark as to this latest acquisition.

As soon as Justyn saw them, he began to sputter. "That is Sara's livestock. What are they doing here? Didn't you think our mutual building project for them was good enough to see them through the winter?"

The attempt at making a joke to cover his confusion sounded lame even to Justyn's ears. However, Lars had picked up the sharpness in his tone.

The somewhat shocked response on Lars' face made Justyn even more confused.

"I thought you knew and had first choice at them" Lars began a little defensively.

"Knew what?" Justyn fired right back, a foreboding thought already beginning to form in his mind.

"Well that Sara and Corrie sold out and moved on" came the dreaded response.

"They did what?" Justyn demanded, his mind not really wanting to go there.

"Yah, sold off what they could and left the rest for the bank to sell. It all happened in a great big hurry. I was mighty surprised too, but thought perhaps tongues had started wagging in town again about Sara or something. Leastwise, she didn't seem to want to talk about her reasons for leaving. I wanted to respect her choice and bought her remaining stock just to help her out. She has been a good neighbor and sister in the Lord."

The long monologue had about worn out the normally quiet farmer.

"Do you have any idea where they went?" The question came out a little strangled as Justyn tried to talk around the huge lump in his throat.

"Not sure" Lars responded quietly. "Like I said, I was trying to mind my own business. But lets go in and talk to the wife over coffee. Maybe Sara confided in her."

The two men made their way to the house, pausing to shake the fresh snow from their boots. It was obvious one was stooped from hard work and age, and the other with a mighty burden, newly planted.

Unfortunately, Lilly Brown could add little more to the story. She did remember a comment about Edmonton or Calgary but even with her, things had been left unusually vague. Both of the Browns were amazed, even shocked, that Justyn had no prior knowledge about his close neighbors' sudden disappearance.

After a quick coffee, Justyn drove on into town to check with Pastor Alden to see if he knew anything about the mysterious exodus. But Pastor was just as surprised by the news as Justyn had been and he was also equally disappointed that Sara had not confided in him, or any other church person, as to her need to leave. How could she have missed that church people were there for one another? Had the gossip started up again, even in the church? Or was something even more sinister going on? As they parted ways, each man's musings continued on their own.

That night at supper Justyn was so depressed that even Amanda, a relative stranger, noticed something was wrong. She really tried to mind her own business but when their already sporadic conversation ended in dead silence for the third time because of Justyn's preoccupation, she finally gently asked, "Is something troubling you Mr. Smyth? You seem like you are carrying the world on your shoulders tonight. Is there something I can do to help?"

Although she asked the questions very politely, Justyn simply shrugged and shook his head no. Almost as an afterthought, he mumbled, "Why do you ask?"

Trying to keep things light, she remarked, "Well, maybe its because you haven't smiled since we got here; or you refuse to look at me while we are talking, or you are not even trying to carry on a conversation and then there is the fact that you keep pushing your food around on your plate without eating any of it."

Still not eliciting a smile, the twinkle in her eye faded and a very serious look replaced it. "Have I . . . Have I done something to offend you?" That silent plea was in her voice again like when they had first met; her insecurity clearly showing through.

Her need for affirmation and care was just what was needed to jerk Justyn back to the present. Godly compassion again replaced the coldness in his gray eyes and he made a special point of smiling at her to reassure her.

"I just learned today that a dear friend of mine suddenly left town without saying goodbye. I'm still in shock I guess" he finished rather lamely.

"Well if he left in a hurry, it can't be for long. They will be back before you know it; just wait and see." Amanda tried to sound reassuring resulting in that upside down way of the child trying to be the strong one for the adult.

Justyn sighed heavily and decided to divulge a little more information. "First of all, the he is a she. Her name is Sara. With her daughter Corrie, she lived on the farm next to me, my closest neighbor." He refrained from saying just how close. "And secondly," he continued, "it appears that they have moved away permanently, not just left for a visit."

Seeing his crestfallen demeanor, Amanda was beginning to get the picture a little more clearly that Justyn realized or was letting on. She had seen men come and go in her mother's life often enough to recognize the initial "can't talk, can't eat" symptoms.

"You love her, this close neighbor Sara, don't you?" It was more an observation then a question, stated gently rather than judgmentally.

Her keen insight from what seemed like so few clues caught Justyn off guard and he could only nod his head in assent, probably admitting the truth to himself as much as to her.

"Did you tell her you love her?" came the next caring question, so full of compassion that Justyn was not threatened in the least to open up.

"Well, not in so many words, I suppose." He couldn't really look her in the eye as he spoke. Something about his fingers down on the table seemed to hold his fascination. "I mean she knew I was fond of her" he said rather defensively now. "She should have known I love her."

Suddenly a soft but warm little hand reached out to grasp and still his quivering, calloused one.

"My Mom made that same mistake. She told me a hundred times that she should never have let you go without clearly telling you how she felt about you. But with the drinking and the drugs, she just drifted away and never even tried to go back to you." There was a catch in her voice as she spoke barely above a whisper, though no one else was anywhere near them. "Don't make the same grave mistake my mother did" she finished. "Don't loose the best thing that has ever happened to you." There were tears in her eyes now. "Go after her, Justyn" she insisted.

At first Justyn just blinked, and then he blinked again. What she just said finally registered. Of course! It was so obvious! Why hadn't he thought about it himself? Here it took a near stranger, and a kid at that, to keep him from making the worst mistake of his life by doing nothing.

"Sara and her daughter Corrie, who is about you age, are very special to me and you are exactly right. I need to go after them as soon as I can find out in which direction they went. Thank you for helping me see what I was just to numb to see." Now tears shown in his eyes too.

Mindless of what other people in the restaurant might think, Justyn jumped up and gently gathered her into his arms and tenderly held her for a moment or two. When the waitress returned, he awkwardly let her go and tried not to act embarrassed.

"Anything else for you and your 'guest' Mr. Smyth?" Donna asked, clearly suggesting there may be a whole other part to their relationship.

"No, I guess that is about it. Just the bill please" Justyn stammered.

While she fished for it in her apron pocket, Amanda suddenly had an inspiration.

"Do you know most of the girls around here our age?" she asked Donna in a conspiring tone.

"Well it's a pretty small town so I suppose I do" the waitress responded back a little cautiously, while placing the bill on the table by Justyn.

Edging up to the front of her seat, Amanda continued sweetly, "I'm trying to find a girl named Corrie. Do you know how I might get a hold of her?"

A look of shock and then defensiveness crossed Donna's face. "Sorry, you are too late. She just moved away." Stopping abruptly after this curt response, Donna tried to make a hasty exit.

"Well, do you have any idea where she moved to?" Amanda persisted by stepping in front of her before Donna could make her escape.

"She said something about her Mom and her trying to make a new start in Edmonton, and then if that didn't work out, maybe trying Calgary" came the begrudging response.

"Any idea why they left so abruptly?" Justyn jumped into the conversation, seeking to hold Donna for even one more minute longer.

"Last I spoke with Corrie was when I told her your daughter here had arrived in town and I wondered if your wife was coming too" Donna divulged in innocence. "Next thing I knew someone said they saw them at the bus depot with their bags packed. Corrie always was a little different." The last was said over her shoulder as Donna sidestepped Amanda and went to wait on another customer who had just come in.

For a second time in the same day, Justyn was again bowled over with a relative tiny bit of news. In a total daze as he paid the bill, Justyn stumbled out the door after Amanda, not really seeing where he was going.

"They knew all along!" Justyn moaned as they settled into his pickup. "And I didn't even go over to try and explain everything!" He angrily hit the steering wheel and probably would have cursed if Amanda hadn't been sitting there. "I can't believe they didn't have more faith in me than that!" The last statement burst out angrier than he intended but he didn't notice until he saw that Amanda's face, right beside him, had turned ashen.

"It's all my fault," she whispered, her whole body quivering. "They left because of me!" and she began to sob. For the second time that morning Justyn gathered her into his arms and they wept together in the relative privacy of the truck.

"So I simply will need to help you find them again," she finally forced the words out around her tears, saying it with such fiery determination that Justyn had to sit back and look at her face.

"You are going to what?" he asked incredulously, his eyes searching hers.

Now that her mind was made up, a plan had begun formulating. "I will go back to Edmonton and look for them. After all, it is my home. I know my way around" she stated matter-of-factly.

"But Edmonton is a huge city of over two hundred thousand people. You wouldn't stand a chance of finding them. Where would you even begin to look?" The hopelessness of the task was already making Justyn feel totally overwhelmed.

But Amanda had already thought of that. "That's easy," she immediately chimed in. "I'll start with the bus depot. I'll just arrive the same way they did and ask around until I find some clues to their trail." She was starting to get excited now. "And if you can give me a picture of them, that I can show around, I'm sure someone will remember seeing them" she enthused, the tears all but forgotten, except for the moisture still on her cheeks.

Justyn was beginning to see just a little light at the end of his dark tunnel of being overwhelmed. His mind jumped to the picture taken of them at the last church picnic.

"You know, we just might have a chance at that. They only just left. People would have to remember them!" The excitement was definitely contagious.

"Excuse me, but did you say 'we'?" Amanda stammered, scarcely believing her ears.

"Yah, I'll come too and we will look together." He said it as though it was the most logical thing in the world.

"But your ranch; your animals . . ." Amanda's voice trailed off, her emotions a mixture of relief and unbelief.

"I can find someone to look after the stock for a few days, even a week or more if needed." Now it was Justyn's mind that was clicking right along. "The point is I am not letting you go searching for them all by yourself in a huge city, even if you do live there. Parts of it just wouldn't be safe and I'm not about to lose you now too" he finished with added authority that surprised them both.

And at that moment of deep felt honesty, a father/daughter bond was fanned into flame, with or without actual bloodlines. And that fresh bond was soon to be sorely tested, as life moved from the sleepy town of Valleyview to the hectic, bustling of city life in Edmonton. Were the four of them actually meant to be one family?

Choice and Consequence

Vic Lehman